Wonder Show

★ ★ ★

Wonder Show

BY

HANNAH BARNABY

Houghton Mifflin Books for Children
HOUGHTON MIFFLIN HARCOURT
Boston New York 2012

Houghton Mifflin Books for Children is an imprint of
Houghton Mifflin Harcourt Publishing Company.

www.hmhbooks.com

The text of this book is set in Horley Old Style MT.

Library of Congress Cataloging-in-Publication Data is on file.

ISBN 978-0-547-59980-9

Manufactured in the United States of America
DOC 10 9 8 7 6 5 4 3
4500398077

FOR THE LOST AND THE LONELY,
FOR THE DIFFERENT AND THE SAME

The Banshee of Brewster Falls

Wayward can mean a lot of things. It can mean lost, misled, unfortunate, left behind. That is how the girls at The Home thought of themselves, despite their best efforts to live some other way.

For the inhabitants of Brewster Falls, *wayward* meant wicked. Dangerous. Trash. And that is how they treated the girls on the rare occasions they showed their faces in town.

Portia was the only one who went on a regular basis—she did the shopping and stopped at the post office for letters and telegrams. She rode the red bicycle and did not cover her long dark hair, and she sang old gypsy songs at the top of her lungs, and she seemed (to the residents of Brewster Falls) like a banshee coming to steal their souls. Mothers would hide their children indoors when Portia came whipping down the road.

They were a fearful group of folks.

Portia loved to torment them. And she loved the red bicycle.

Riding a bicycle was the only kind of freedom for Portia. It was something she thought she'd always known how to do, simply because she couldn't remember learning, couldn't place the first time she'd done it. Like laughing. Or eating an apple. It was so utterly normal that it didn't even require thought. Settle onto the seat. Push off, pedal, right left right left right. Hold the handle-bars steady. Watch the road ahead, to avoid cars and potholes and squirrels, but don't look too hard at anything. She could almost get out of her body, almost pretend she was entirely somewhere else.

That was the freedom she loved. That was why she had worked so hard to convince Mister to let her take the trips to town, be-cause it afforded her the luxury of time alone on her bicycle.

Only it wasn't her bicycle—it was Mister's. It had been his since a Christmas morning once upon a time, when a little boy who would grow up to be Mister had tumbled out of bed and found a string tied to his left big toe, a string that he untied and followed out of his room, through the upstairs hallway to the stairs, down the stairs (unwinding it carefully from the banister), through the dining room, into the kitchen (such a long string!), and through the side door, which he opened to find a shiny red Journeyman five-speed leaning against the porch rail.

Was he happy? Did he gasp with delight? Or did he stand there with a hand full of string and think, *They don't know me at all*?

It hardly matters, now.

PART ONE

BEGIN AT THE BEGINNING

Stories came easily to Portia. Lies came even more easily, and more often. The difference was in the purpose. The stories taught her to imagine places beyond where she was, and the lies kept her out of trouble. Mostly.

Portia's first audience, for lies and stories both, was her father. Her mother had never had the ear for tales of any kind, nor the patience to listen, and she was long gone by the time Portia could tell a tale. A lean, restless woman, Quintillia surprised no one with her departure, and the family quickly closed the space she had occupied like the ocean fills a hole in the sand. They did not speak of her. If they ever thought of her, it was in silence.

And so it was Max, her father, who listened to Portia talk, talk, talk. Out the door, around the house, all the way to the woodpile and back, the sound of Portia's voice trailed Max like an echo. She had an uncanny way of matching her rhythms to his, tailoring her stories to his moods and whatever task he worked on while she talked. They were stream-of-conscious-ness ramblings at first, retellings of the fairy tales Portia heard from her gypsy tribe of relations, all of whom lived within spitting distance of her bedroom window and congregated nightly in Aunt Carmella's kitchen on the other side of the vegetable garden. Portia did not have to leave her room to hear them speaking at night—they knew she was there and projected their voices accordingly. She made the stories her own, chopped them up and clapped them back together in new formations, putting the enchanted princess in the loving embrace of a villainous wolf, marrying the charming prince to the wicked witch and giving them a brood of dwarfs to raise as their own.

Sometimes Portia would have so many storied roads in her head that she would struggle to choose just one path. "Papa," she said, "I can't tell where this story begins."

"Begin at the beginning," he told her.

These were the earliest days Portia would remember later. Trying to think past them, to drill into her younger selves and mine them for memories, she could get only as far as the view from that bedroom window, the sound of her shadowed aunts and uncles laughing, telling tales, and singing songs about women Portia knew not to repeat in polite company.

These were the days before the money dried up and the dust took over, before the jobs and houses were lost, before her tribe disbanded and went away like seeds on the wind, hoping to find a place where they could land safely.

As her family trickled away, Portia replaced the stories they had told with stories of her own. She didn't like the feeling of their words in her mouth anymore; besides, the details began to fade, and it seemed her father smiled only when she told her own tales.

"There are creatures that dance outside my window at

night," she told him, "and they are very fat. They have wings, but they cannot fly because their wings are too small."

"What do they sound like?" asked Max.

"Like bees," said Portia.

"What do they want?" asked Max.

"To fly," said Portia. "They want to fly, more than anything."

"What are their names?" asked Max.

The only names Portia knew were the names of her lost relatives. She had not been to school. She did not have friends or know anyone who was not her family. She was five years old.

"Their names are Carmella and Joseph and Anthony and Oscar and Elena and . . ." Then she stopped because a tear pushed itself out of Max's eye, and the sight of it rolling down her father's face made Portia feel that she had done something very wrong.

"Papa," she whispered. "It's not true."

"I know," said Max.

"Then why are you sad?"

"Because our family is gone," he said. "I didn't think they could fly, but they did."

Portia put her hand into her father's coat pocket, where his own hand rested like a nesting bird. "If they flew away, they can fly back," she said.

Max shrugged. "Or we will fly away, too."

Of course Portia thought *we* included her.

She was five years old.

CIRCUS

A few weeks after Portia turned nine, Max and Aunt Sophia took her to the circus, to distract her from the empty houses and the dust and the quiet. It was Max's idea, the circus, but it was Sophia's money that got them in. She grumbled a bit as she handed it over to the beaming woman in the ticket wagon, but even Sophia wasn't immune to the alluring smells of sawdust and pink sugar that hung all around them. Even she had been a child once.

They went through the menagerie at first, gaping at elephants and the one colossal hippo that bobbed calmly in a huge tank of water. Max moved quickly, wanting to see everything at once, turning occasionally to glance at his daughter behind him. Portia stood next to Sophia and resisted the urge to grab her hand when one of the elephants extended its trunk in her direction, the fleshy tip trembling as it searched the air.

"I think it's looking for a kiss," Sophia said. Her voice was high-pitched, full of forced excitement. It made Portia glad she had kept her hands at her sides.

When they exited the tent at the other end of the menagerie, they found themselves on the midway. There was a long row of booths on each side, selling popcorn and cotton candy and chances to throw things to win other things. Portia knew better than to ask if she could play one of the games — Max might have relented, but Aunt Sophia was against gambling of any kind and would have spent the rest of the day lecturing Portia on the subject. Though it would almost have been a relief to hear Sophia speaking in her normal voice instead of her false, cheery day-at-the-circus one.

Halfway down the east side of the midway, between the ring toss and the Beano booth, was a long stage with a squat tent behind it. There was a podium at one end, next to the tent entrance, and a huge sign above the stage that said STRANGE PEOPLE.

The crowd was dense. Portia couldn't see the stage, but she could hear the tinny strains of accordion music over the murmuring voices that wove their way back to her.

"What's that?" she asked. Max was silent, and Portia felt chastened. She had been asking too many questions lately, and Max no longer had any answers. Or had become, like her mother, unwilling to share them. Sophia — who was taller than most of the women in the crowd and a good number of the men, too — looked down at Portia disapprovingly. "Nothing that concerns you. Let's go."

"But what is it? I can't see!"

A large man next to Sophia leaned down to Portia and said, "You can't see? Well, that won't do. Here, let me help." She was small for her age — it took no effort at all for the man to reach down and lift Portia as if she were a bag of groceries and plunk her down onto his shoulders. Sophia sputtered a bit, but she lived by "good manners above all" and couldn't bring herself to reprimand a total stranger.

Portia's newfound height gave her a perfect view, but even though she could see the figure on the stage, she still wasn't sure what she was looking at. It seemed to be a man, but he didn't look like any man Portia had ever seen. His head was very small and bald and rather pointy at the back, and his face seemed too big. It was sloped as though someone had grabbed his nose and pulled everything down toward his nearly absent chin.

Accidentally out loud, Portia said, "What is it?"

"It's The Pinhead," the man told her.

"Is he . . . What's wrong with him?"

"Don't know," said the man. "But he sure is funny-looking, ain't he?"

The Pinhead smiled peacefully as he played his accordion and gazed down at the stage. He did not look into the audience, and everyone stared and whispered as if he were on a movie screen instead of right there in front of them. Finally, he finished his song with a little flourish and, still smiling, shuffled off the stage, slipping behind a hidden opening in the tent canvas.

Another man stepped up to the podium. He was wearing a white suit, so white in the early afternoon sun that Portia had to shield her eyes to look at him.

"Ladies and gentlemen," he called, "let's hear a big round of applause for Gregor, last surviving member of the lost tribe of Montezuma."

There was a smattering of hesitant applause, and the white-suit man went on.

"And now, ladies and gentlemen, our main event. This is what your friends and neighbors will be talking about long after our humble show is gone from your fine town. You will tell your grandchildren the story of this day, and they will scarcely believe you, it is so fantastic. Seeing is believing, but you will not believe your eyes."

He paused and put his hand in the air.

"Ladies and gentlemen, I present to you: The Gallery of Human Oddities."

Portia looked down at her father, to see what he was making of all this, but Max wasn't looking at the stage. Instead, he was staring past one side of it, fixing his eyes on something far away.

Sophia tapped Portia's benefactor on the shoulder. "Excuse me, sir, but I think I should take my niece to a more . . . suitable part of the show."

"Of course," he said. He lifted Portia from around his neck and set her carefully on the ground.

"But—"

"What do you say?" Sophia snapped.

"Thank you, sir," Portia said to the man, and he tipped his hat.

Portia jogged to keep up with Sophia, who was striding swiftly toward the biggest tent on the lot. Max floated distractedly behind her. "Why couldn't we stay and watch?"

"It's not appropriate," Sophia said.

"*What's* not appropriate?" Portia's mind was swimming

with what it was she'd seen, what the white-suit man could have meant by "human oddities," why Aunt Sophia was practically running away from the midway stage.

"The sideshow," Sophia said. "No more questions."

There was no better way to ensure Portia's obsession with something than telling her to forget about it.

She was distracted a bit as the circus performance began. Portia had never seen such things outside of her imagination: girls hanging by their hair and turning somersaults, small stocky men throwing themselves into the air and catching each other by the wrists, massive tigers obeying the whip-snap commands of the fearless woman who stood inside their cage. Girls riding horses standing up, bears on bicycles, elephants dancing like ballerinas. It was enchanting, like a fairy tale come to life.

But for all the whirling colors and motion and noise, all Portia could think about was what she had *not* been allowed to see. And that night her dreams were filled with new characters—a man with the head of a bear; a woman the size of a zeppelin, hovering overhead; an army of accordion-playing pinheads—as she tried to figure out what stories might have been hiding behind the curtain on the midway, waiting just for her.

It was barely another week before Max determined that it was time to go. In the years to come, Portia's memories of the circus would become hopelessly tangled with the image of her father driving away, so that it eventually seemed clear to her that Max had gone to follow the circus. His distant silence during their outing became, in Portia's mind, a symptom of deep fascination with the midway, the menagerie, and that mysterious tent she had not been allowed to enter. As actual memories faded, they were replaced by dreamlike pictures of Max as a lion tamer, a roustabout, a ringmaster.

Max and the circus were united for good.

And then they both vanished.

GONE

When he finally departed, her father said the same things her aunts and uncles and cousins all had said. "I will come back for you." "This is not goodbye." "This is our only chance." And the last thing, always: "Be brave." Someone always said that. This time it was Max.

"Don't tell me that," Portia whispered, and Max looked suitably ashamed. He should have known better, she thought. He should have given her something of his own to keep.

"It won't be long," he said softly. He said it into the air above Portia's head, like a blessing over her. Like a prayer.

"As long as it takes," Sophia told Max. "I'm not going anywhere."

Max made himself believe her. He kissed Portia one more time and climbed into his truck. Portia angrily rubbed her cheek as the motor started, wiping Max's kiss away, and then immediately regretted it when she saw his pained expression in the rearview mirror as he drove away.

There were no other children her age around anymore, so Portia was the only one there with Aunt Sophia. She was the only one who stood in the road and choked on the dust that rose up behind her father's truck, the only one who cried dirty tears that night (unless Sophia cried, too, which was very hard to imagine). She was the last storyteller in her haunted forest, and Aunt Sophia was an unkind audience.

"Nonsense," she barked. "All that stuff about goblins and trolls. Your mind is ridiculous, Portia."

"Don't you believe in monsters?" Portia asked.

"I believe in bears," Sophia replied, "and I believe in the devil."

"Those aren't monsters."

"You face them down and then tell me that."

Portia imagined her barrel-shaped Aunt Sophia doing battle with the devil and an army of bears, and then thought better of asking if such an event had ever taken place. Even if it had, Sophia would never tell her about it. Aunt Sophia didn't believe in stories. She believed in practical knowledge, in cooking, in planting a garden, in survival. She believed in staying where God had put her, which was why she agreed to hold on to Portia until Max returned.

Sophia had meant what she said.

She wasn't going anywhere.

PORTIA

Papa said he didn't want to leave but he had to. Whenever I didn't want to do something but I had to, it was because Aunt Sophia made me. So I asked Papa who was making him leave, and he said, "Money," and I got angry because money isn't a person, it's a thing, so he wasn't answering my question.

Then Papa went to pack up the truck, and he hugged me real tight and said, "I'm gonna miss you so much, little bug," and I made him let me go because I wasn't little anymore. I was nine. And he should have known better.

I think Papa left because there was no more whiskey, and no more music at night. There was plenty of work to do, and we could have done it together. I would have helped, I wouldn't have argued when Papa asked me to do anything. Even if it was something hard like mend the latch on the sheep pen. But it wouldn't have been that because there were no more sheep, either.

I told myself: Papa went to find the sheep and bring them back to me.

I am going to wait for him every day.

I am going to be a good girl for Aunt Sophia.

I am going to learn new stories for when Papa comes back.

And I am never going to stop waiting.

THE APPLE TREE

It was where Portia did her best waiting, under the apple tree. The tree was not very big, and she liked that because so many places made her feel smaller than she wanted to be. She was shaded from sun and rain there. There was a curve in the trunk that fit against her back like another body, and it helped her remember what it was like to be held, to be safe.

Aunt Sophia did not hold her. Aunt Sophia took care of her, fed her, kept her clean and dry. Taught her what Aunt Sophia knew how to teach: manners, churchgoing, and cooking.

There were always apples on the ground, with soft brown spots from falling and sitting still too long. Portia bit into one once, one that looked more perfect than the others, but it did not taste like an apple. It was hard and bitter. She spit out the bite she'd taken and laid the rest of the apple back on the ground, bite side down, so it looked perfect again.

If she lay against the trunk of the tree and looked up through the branches, she could see only bits of the sky and the clouds passing over the leaves like a moving picture made just for her. When the road was too empty to watch anymore, Portia had this other view to comfort her. When, after a while, that was not enough, she knew it was time to go back inside.

She was careful with her apple tree. She did not ask too much of it.

WHILE I WAS WAITING
(FROM THE NOTEBOOK OF PORTIA REMINI)

A partial list of things that happened <u>accidentally</u> in the year I lived with Aunt Sophia:

1. A small fire involving dining room curtains and candles during an attempted séance to call forth the ghost of William Howard Taft.

2. A disagreement as to the meaning of the word <u>disagreement</u> between myself and one Miss Eugenia Throgsmorton, Head-mistress, Sutton County Day School.

3. The loss of an entire batch of newly carded wool, which was left outdoors during a rather exciting thunderstorm.

4. The acquisition of a mild case of influenza, resulting from the exploration of waist-deep sinkholes in the midst of said thunderstorm.

And the following incidents, which took place in church:

1. Daring escape by mouse from pocket of my dress.

2. Similar escape by salamander—same pocket, different Sunday.

3. So-called defacement of prayer missals, in which certain words were altered in unsavory directions.

4. Unfortunate misfire of pea from peashooter, leading to the removal of pea from Miss Eugenia Throgsmorton's ear.

All of the above were completely unintentional, not to mention unfairly punished.

Broken Promise

Aunt Sophia was a hard spirit. She had survived her life because of a stalwart, stubborn refusal to change. Some women are that way, no matter how many sons they lose in a war, no matter how hard they must work after their husbands are carelessly dispatched by a hay baler, no matter how many troublesome girls they take in. Women like Sophia are great rocks in the sea, weathered and worn but never broken.

When Portia first went to live with Sophia, she thought she would not let herself be changed, either. Portia thought she would be in Aunt Sophia's house only for a short time. She did not know that her father would go down that open road and not return on any of the days she stood at the front gate and watched until she saw trailing black spots from staring so hard. She thought she should be the first to see him coming, so she gave up climbing trees and writing down stories and doing all the things she loved. She only watched the road. Finally Aunt Sophia got fed up and dragged Portia into the house, and she didn't stop even when Portia kicked her in the stomach.

I hate her, Portia told herself. But even then she knew it wasn't true. Aunt Sophia taught her how to cook and sew, and she let her read any book Portia wanted as long as she spent the same amount of time reading the Bible, which was fine with Portia because the Bible has more than its fair share of gory tales and intrigue.

Portia once imagined herself as David, with Sophia playing Goliath, and saw herself land that stone directly between Sophia's eyes so that she dropped dead immediately. Then Portia felt terribly guilty and washed all of Aunt Sophia's unmentionables without complaining once.

Did David feel so guilty? After he killed Goliath, did he gently bathe his gigantic body with a wet rag tied to a very long stick? No, he did not.

It is a terrible curse for a storyteller, to have such a conscience.

"As long as it takes," Sophia told Max. "I'm not going anywhere."

And she didn't go anywhere. But Portia did.

Four years after her father was swallowed in a cloud of dust, Portia turned thirteen, and the old family traits were in full bloom. She was willful, stubborn, and prone to daydreams. She was clumsy. She was emotional. She was, in fact, exactly like her Uncle Hiram, who had been Sophia's husband and the bane of her existence until he got himself crushed by the hay baler. ("Head in the clouds" was all Sophia said when the men came to tell her the news. She was not the least bit surprised to find herself a widow. Nor was she particularly upset.)

Sophia decided the best thing for everyone was to install Portia in a place where she would be safe, disciplined, and out of Sophia's way.

Like an oasis in the desert, there was The Home.

"Pack your things," Sophia said to Portia. They had just finished dinner.

"Why?"

"I've found a better place for you to live. There are lots of other girls there, and an apple orchard, and a very nice man who will watch after you. Here. Look."

Sophia stood up, went to her sewing box, and extracted a thin slip of paper. As she pushed it across the table, Portia could see a faint picture of a large house surrounded by bold words in newsprint. Words like BETTER LIFE and CARE and HOME. The words smudged her fingers as she pinched the paper between them.

Portia felt her scalp getting hot. When she looked up, she could see her apple tree through the window behind Sophia. "You're sending me away?"

"It's for the best, dear. You'll be much happier there. You'll get an education."

It was as if her hair were actually on fire. She itched at her head and said, "But you promised Max you would take care of me. He's coming back here to get me. I'm supposed to be *here*."

Sophia folded her hands together tightly. "There's . . . he . . ." She paused, chewing on her words. "I will tell him where to find you. Obviously. And I *am* taking care of you. I have found a better place for you." She stood up, hands clenched as if in desperate prayer. "Now, pack your things. We're leaving in the morning."

I'll run away, thought Portia. But there was no time to plan, and she knew only fools fled into the night without the proper supplies. She had heard too many tales of men mauled by bears, getting lost in the woods, sleeping their way into death when the snow caught them. She would not suffer that kind of end. She would not give Sophia the satisfaction.

A whole orchard of apple trees. Other girls to climb them with. A kindly man, watching over them like the Holy Father. Portia pictured a friendly, wrinkled face, a snow white beard, a pipe threading sweet smoke into the air. A deep voice telling her stories, tucking her in at night.

Maybe it won't be so bad, she thought. And when she woke up in the middle of the night and heard Aunt Sophia yelling in her sleep, Portia smiled and thought, *So long, you old witch.*

She didn't know yet: There are far worse things than witches. Worse than bears. Worse than the devil himself.

Meeting Mister

They drove for nearly two hours before they got to Brewster Falls. It was the longest trip Portia had ever taken.

Aunt Sophia didn't like for anyone to speak to her while she was driving, and so she and Portia made the journey in silence, except for the constant rattling of the ancient truck that had been left behind by some near-forgotten cousin. Portia entertained herself with visions of the kindly old man who awaited her, and his pipe and the bedtime stories she hoped to hear — her stock of stories was wearing thin, and she couldn't tell them to herself without hearing Max's voice.

Her hopeful imaginings started to sag when they drove through Brewster Falls and it looked exactly like all the other towns they'd gone through already. Portia was suddenly suspicious that Sophia had been driving in circles and this had all been an elaborate trick to scare Portia into behaving better. But then she saw the sign:

MCGREAVEY HOME FOR WAYWARD GIRLS

Block letters burned into the wood like scars.

"What does *wayward* mean?"

Sophia coughed. "It means you've strayed from the right-eous path."

For all the times she'd been dragged to church, Portia didn't think she'd ever been on the righteous path in the first place. She did not imagine that Brother Joshua — unearthly tall and thin, with a waxed mustache and a crooked smile — was at all qualified to lead anyone to Righteousness. Even Sophia seemed not to trust him and pursed her lips when he clasped her hand at the end of services every Sunday. But the real preachers had all joined the westbound caravans, and beggars could not be choosers. Even in God's house.

The truck lurched uncertainly onto the dirt road indicated by the sign and quickly came to a fork — downhill, to the right, Portia saw a cluster of small wood cabins and, behind them, the apple trees. They were different than her apple tree. Hers had grown tall and sat heavy over her like a canopy, even now that she was thirteen. These were dwarfish, twisted, and gray. It was halfway through harvest time, and many of the trees stood bare as skeletons, reaching for the cold sky. Uphill, to the left, was a massive dark house with a sharp, staggered roof that looked like the teeth of some huge, mythical beast. Portia had no desire to get any closer, but Sophia, as usual, had other ideas.

"That must be where the director lives," she said, and aimed the truck accordingly. When they pulled up in front of the house, the door opened as if by magic, and a man stepped onto the porch.

He was thin, with well-trimmed black hair and the bearing of a man who believes himself taller than he actually is. His suit was a cold gray, like slate, and there was no expression on his pale face. He matched the house perfectly—his eyes were as black as the shaded windows behind him. He stood with his hands behind his back and waited.

Sophia heaved herself out of the truck and approached the man. "You are the director?"

The man nodded, drew one hand from behind him, and extended it to Sophia. "You must be Mrs. Stoller. Charmed, I'm sure."

He did not sound charmed at all. He sounded, in fact, like a man who had never been charmed by anything or anyone in his life.

"You received my letter?"

"I did," he said.

Sophia pulled a handkerchief from her sleeve and ran it through her hands like a rosary. "Portia's not a bad girl, you understand, it's just that I can't—"

"Of course," he said.

Sophia sighed heavily and only then noticed that Portia was still sitting in the truck. "Come on now," she said, her voice heavy with forced sweetness.

Portia did not move.

"Yes, come now, Portia," the man purred. "Come out and meet your new friends."

At that, two girls in dark dresses emerged from the side of the house and approached the truck. They stared at her through the open window. One of them smiled. The other ducked her head so that her long yellow hair draped her face like water closing around a stone in a riverbed.

"Portia," Sophia hissed. "Now."

Slowly, Portia reached for the door handle, pulled it, swung the door open, and stepped into the strange new air. From one corner of the porch, a rusted, empty birdcage shuddered and creaked in the breeze.

"The girls will show you to your quarters," said the man.

The smiling one reached into the back of the truck and retrieved Portia's bag. "This way," she said, and started down the path to the orchard and the bunkhouses. Portia glanced at Sophia, who waved her hand impatiently as she turned back to the dark man and began to speak low words that Portia could not hear.

The yellow-haired girl looked at Portia for a long moment, and then she whispered, "It's harder if you put up a fight. Just come." She put out her hand, and Portia didn't know what else to do but put her own hand in the girl's palm and follow her. And their hands stayed together as they walked to the dingy bunkhouse that smelled like rotten apples, as they sat on a lumpy bed with scratchy blankets, as a swarm of sad-eyed girls surrounded them.

And it wasn't until Portia heard Sophia's truck driving away that the girl said, "My name is Caroline."

FAMILY TRADITIONS

Family recipes must be kept in your head, Aunt Sophia told Portia once. They are not for writing down.

But Portia liked to write things down. She was very fond of her own handwriting, and she liked the way everything looked when she wrote it out. When she went back to read what she'd written before, it was as if everything were her idea.

So she spent part of her modest allowance (which she awarded to herself from Aunt Sophia's purse) on notebooks and pencils. And she wrote down Aunt Sophia's recipes and stories she imagined, and over and over again she wrote what she could remember.

Her mother in a blue coat with a furry collar.

The soap smell on Max's neck.

Knock-knock jokes.

Aunts in red lipstick and rose perfume, uncles in suspenders and whiskey.

It wasn't much and also Portia wasn't sure if she was really remembering these things or if she was simply writing what she had written before. Still. She kept writing, kept stealing dimes from Aunt Sophia for notebooks and pencils.

The notebooks were the first thing Mister took away.

NIGHT VOICES

The one inside Portia said:

"It's cold here and everything smells like apples."

It said, "I hope Aunt Sophia has one of her headaches right now."

It said, "How will Papa find me?"

The ones outside, in the wind and the rustling orchard, said:

"Now you belong to us."

They said, "No one is coming for you.

And you know it."

BLUEBEARD

The Home was a giant on the hill, towering over the bunk-houses, all angles and dark dead window eyes. Mister's resemblance to it made a certain amount of sense, because he hardly ever left it.

Mister liked having girls work for him. Long ago, when his mother was alive and still spry enough to enjoy a good party, there had been servants who were trained to run the household like a business: efficiently, quietly, and without crisis. On the day of his mother's funeral Mister gave each of the servants an envelope with a terse letter of recommendation and a small sum of money and sent them packing. He saw no reason to employ professionals. Not when there was a population of girls so conveniently located at the bottom of the hill.

The Home, too, had been his mother's idea. A pet project, a personal charity that would (she had hoped) endear her to the people of Brewster Falls. She had pictured herself as a guardian angel, a patron saint. In the end, she failed to obtain endorsement of the church and the entire enterprise had backfired, for she was ultimately seen as the woman who sought to populate the town with young ladies of questionable character and perhaps even loose morals. The young men in town were delighted at first, but soon they turned on her as well, after seeing that the girls who came to The Home were just like the girls they already knew, only without parents or spending money or decent clothes.

It was precisely these deficiencies that Mister preyed on when recruiting the girls for his household staff, by promising pocket change and the chance to win their way back into the hearts of the families who had sent them here. Of course, not every girl was convinced. Portia, for instance, was sure that Mister had no real desire to help any of his charges and had about as much chance of redeeming her as he did of sprouting a pair of wings and flying south for the winter.

On the other hand, Portia was very curious about a few things, such as the contents of her personal file. The girls liked to speculate about these files, carefully stored in a secret place in the big house, cradling all sorts of vital information. Parents' names, addresses, correspondence. Dates of release. The files became invisible security blankets, something to hold at night and soothe their minds, which buzzed and hummed like machines. Some girls who had been inside the house, for work or discipline, reported seeing marked papers and such on Mister's desk, but since none of them had ever had the courage to touch anything in his office, they could not attest to the files' contents. Portia doubted the credibility of these girls, as she doubted nearly everything she heard. But she reasoned that *if* the files existed, and *if* she could get her hands on them, she *might* find something useful. She had always suspected that Sophia had an idea of where Max had gone, though Sophia had always denied it. If she had shared that knowledge with Mister, he would likely have put it in Portia's file.

If there was such a thing.

And the house itself fascinated her, tugged at the same part of her mind as ghost stories and the dime novels she had stolen from the general store and hidden under her mattress at Sophia's. (They had probably been discovered by now.) She cast Mister as Bluebeard, luring girls into his house, locking his secrets away in closets where the dark was thick. She could see the house through a knothole in the cabin wall, and she watched it at night, the frigid winter air breathing back at her, and after some time she would have sworn she saw the house pulsating like a beating heart. Savage. Relentless.

She couldn't wait to get inside.

"What makes you think he's even going to ask you?" Caroline asked. "You're nothing but trouble as far as he's concerned."

"But he likes *you*," said Portia, "and you like me, and if you tell him you won't go without me . . ."

In fact, Mister had already approached Caroline several times and appealed to her, in his noxious way, to come up to the house. He had projects, he said, that involved documenting his family history and his own philosophies on matters of great importance, and he was in need of a smart girl to take dictation and assist in his research. Caroline repeated all of this to Portia, who rolled her eyes and expressed her belief that Mister's reasons for wanting Caroline in the house had very little to do with research. Portia had often seen him watching Caroline from the door of the sewing room, through the trees in the orchard, across the pews during Sunday chapel.

"Why would I tell him that?"

Portia tapped one of Caroline's smooth white hands. "Because you don't want to ruin those with manual labor. Once we're up there, I will do all the cooking and all the cleaning, and all you'll have to do is assist him with his crazy projects. And neither one of us will ever have to pick another goddamned apple or hem another goddamned pair of pants."

A true entrepreneur, Mister had convinced the child welfare authorities that teaching his wards a trade and enabling them to work outdoors would ultimately benefit the girls and aid their "transformation into more productive members of society." This was how sewing mail-order uniforms and harvesting apples in Mister's family orchards had become mandatory for each and every resident of the McGreavey Home for Wayward Girls. Every resident, that is, except for the girls who were appointed to the household staff. And as hard as Caroline tried to sound disinterested, Portia knew exactly how much she hated sewing and picking apples.

"Portia!" Caroline whispered. "Language!"

Portia rolled her eyes. "Whatever way I say it, you know I'm right. We'd be free of this"—she waved her hands like a magician—"and we'd have a nice big roof over our heads again."

Caroline had lived in a large house before. Her family had money and the things that went with money, like feather beds and housekeepers and a deathly fear of scandal, which is why Caroline had been stashed away at The Home when rumors had begun circulating about her and the gardener's son. "Only temporary," Caroline's mother said in all her letters. But it had been almost two years already, and Caroline was beginning to lose hope.

"And," Portia added, "won't your mother be impressed when she hears you've moved from the orchard to the house?"

Portia would later wonder whether she had been playing fair when she said that. There was nothing Caroline wanted more than for her mother to send one last letter calling her home. She prayed for it every night, the cement floor of the bunkhouse pressing her knees until they were numb, and sometimes in the mornings as well. She said her prayers in a near-silent whisper, but once in a while Portia would catch a phrase.

"I'll never see Daniel again," Caroline promised. "I'll do everything my mother says. Please, please, let me go home."

In the end, of course, Caroline's mother did send one last letter. But that was not for several months. And by then the tiny pocket of hope that Caroline carried with her had drained itself empty as a broken hourglass.

And the girls would all remember the version of Bluebeard that Portia had told them as they sewed the hems of relentless numbers of pant legs, the story starring Mister and his mysterious house, and they would shiver like dry leaves.

PORTIA

I may not have been easy to care for, but I was surely not a wayward girl. I knew exactly where I wanted to be, and it wasn't sleeping in a cabin at the bottom of Mister's hill, picking apples from his gnarled trees, sewing uniforms until my fingers went numb, pretending to be grateful because he fed me and put a leaking roof over my head.

Of course, I'd been nothing but a thorn in his side since I'd arrived (a fact that gave me particular pleasure, I confess). I was good at thinking of games for the little girls to play with sticks and apples, which chafed Mister to no end because to him apples equaled money. I told ghost stories and tall tales in the sewing room, and most girls couldn't listen and sew at the same time. And girls not working equaled nothing for Mister's bank account.

I wasn't afraid of him because I thought I had nothing to lose.

I finally talked Caroline into moving up to Mister's, and I wouldn't have believed it possible, but working up there made me miss the bunkhouse. Maybe I'd gotten too used to the sound of a dozen other girls sleeping around me. Or maybe the house had absorbed something of Mister's wicked little soul. He inhabited the place as if it had always been his, as though he would live forever within its steady walls. Like he hadn't crouched in the shadows waiting for his mother to die so he could spring on the carcass of her life and feast on what was left.

Perhaps that sounds a bit dramatic. I have been accused of worse things than embellishing the truth. I am even guilty of some of them.

Whatever my sins, I am no liar. Not anymore. And I tell you true: there was something festering in the heart of that house.

CAROLINE AT NIGHT

They didn't have to share a room. Mister's house had empty spaces to spare. But it had been so long since either of them had slept alone that, without even really discussing it, Portia and Caroline packed their things, carried them up the hill, and moved together into the room at the back corner of the house. It was the only room without a view of the orchard, except for Mister's room, which was at the other end of the upstairs hallway and obviously not an option.

They did not want to look out over their recent past and feel guilty for having escaped it—to think of the other girls sleeping in the frigid, drafty bunkhouses and crying silently for the homes they remembered a little less every day. And spring was slow in coming this year. When they opened the windows in the morning, the thin air still had a cold lining, like snow inside a blanket.

It was only at night that they felt so entirely, insurmountably bleak. Moving into the house did not, as it turned out, spare Portia or Caroline from the nightly misery of time to think. And it was quite some time before Portia was able to begin her search for the legendary files. Mister had a stringent schedule — each day of the week brought its own list of chores — and there was little time for exploration. Plus, he had brought a third girl up from the bunkhouses. Delilah was brash and nosy, talking constantly while Portia tried in vain to tune her out.

"Where'd you come from? Where's your family? Mine's from Decatur, but they headed west a while back. Yours go too? Tell you they'd come back soon? Yep, that's what they told me."

Portia had the distinct feeling that Mister had recruited Delilah to drive her mad.

Whatever comforts Portia and Caroline had expected to find, this house was not their home any more than the orchard or the bunkhouse or the workrooms. So they found ways to distract each other, to calm their minds until sleep managed to overtake them.

Most nights, it went like this:

PORTIA: What are you afraid of?

CAROLINE: Everything.

PORTIA: No, really.

CAROLINE: Really.

PORTIA: How can you be afraid of *everything*?

CAROLINE: In this house, I am.

PORTIA: Are you afraid of me?

CAROLINE: You're not a thing.

PORTIA: What about the rest of the world? What are you afraid of out there?

CAROLINE: Sometimes I think there is no rest of the world. I think this might be all there is.

PORTIA: You know that's not true.

CAROLINE: I can't remember what my mother's voice sounds like. I can't remember how many trees there are in my front yard. Maybe I imagined my whole life before I got here. Maybe it wasn't real.

PORTIA: You're not crazy.

CAROLINE: Promise?

PORTIA: Yes. I promise. Now, pick just one thing to be afraid of. Just one. And the rest can't hurt you.

CAROLINE: One thing?

PORTIA: Yes. One.

CAROLINE: Being alone in the dark.

PORTIA: You're not.

CAROLINE: Not yet.

BLUEBEARD TAKES A BRIDE

Time, as they say, passed. Portia had hoped to spend a few weeks at most in Mister's house — she had envisioned herself moving in and barely unpacking before she seized her magic file and ran off to find Max. Or at least took a few steps in the right direction. But the regimented schedule of housework, cooking, and daily chores, the numbing regularity of life in Mister's house, made time disappear. It was as if some unseen force stole Portia's days and weeks whenever her back was turned. She was washing the kitchen windows one day and was shocked to see alabaster blossoms populating the orchard trees, and her bicycle rides into Brewster Falls no longer required a coat.

The trips to town had been sanctioned by Mister only a few weeks earlier, after much pleading by Portia to Caroline. Portia could not abide asking Mister for such a thing directly, but he had become more and more fond of Caroline in their months of working together and allowed her nearly anything she requested.

Caroline was, of course, repelled by Mister's attention. But Portia reminded her almost daily of the praise that was sure

to come from Caroline's family when they found time to re-
spond to her letters. Caroline wrote to her mother at least twice
a week, detailing her duties as Mister's assistant in his many
intellectual pursuits. In truth, neither Caroline nor Portia was
quite sure what Mister hoped to accomplish by documenting
his lineage, as it was quite clear that no one in Brewster Falls
wanted any association with the McGreavey name. Nor could
they tell what kind of readership Mister might find for his various "doctrines," which were opinionated and difficult to follow, and bore titles like "The Arrogance of Flight" (in which
the actor Howard Hughes was compared to Lucifer). Portia
wondered what a man who had apparently never left his house
could possibly have to say about Hughes's record-breaking
flight around the world, but she listened with great fascination
to Caroline's account of Mister's fierce expression and ever-
reddening countenance as he dictated long sentences that made
no sense to her whatsoever. Many of Mister's opinions seemed
to come, Caroline said, from some inner well of religious conviction. Which, too, seemed strange, since Mister never went
to church, excepting the Sundays when Father Sipperly came
out from town and held services in the decrepit chapel that the
departed Mrs. McGreavey had built in the northeast corner of
the orchard. And he allowed Father Sipperly's visits only in order to avoid any appearance of impropriety.

One man, unmarried, living alone with so many girls. Mister was aware of how it looked.

"I am aware of how it looks," he said to Portia one evening
as he watched her making meat loaf for dinner. He was very
particular about his food and often "supervised" her cooking.
"Perhaps it is time I took a wife."

He said it as if he were talking about acquiring a new mule. Portia was glad her back was turned to him so he could not see her grimace.

"It is only a question of who would be most . . . suitable," he went on. "Not too young, not too headstrong."

This clearly put Portia out of the running, a fact that she celebrated by garnishing the meat loaf with extra parsley. But what Mister said next nearly made her drop the platter altogether.

"I believe I shall speak to Caroline about this. She has become rather . . . dear to me." He spoke absently, trying out the words as he might experiment with some foreign dialect he did not understand. It was as if he had forgotten Portia was there, and she dared not move, dared not remind him. "Yes," he murmured. "I shall speak to her first thing after dinner."

Which gave Portia (in her estimation) just enough time to mash the potatoes, set the table, and convince Caroline to run away.

Except that Caroline didn't want to run away.

And she wasn't surprised to hear that Mister was planning, in his odd way, to propose.

"You said it yourself," Caroline said, "that moving up to the house would show my mother how I've changed. That she'd know for certain that I wasn't in love with Daniel anymore. Just think how well my getting engaged will show her the same thing."

"But," Portia spluttered, "it's *Mister*. You can't be serious. You can't possibly think—"

"All I know is that I haven't heard from my mother in

months. Months, Portia. I have to do something to make her see that I've grown up."

"But you haven't grown up! Not if you think marrying that man is going to help you get home. You'll be trapped here forever. He'll never let you leave."

Caroline waved her hand like she was swatting at an errant bee. "I won't actually have to marry him, silly. Mother would never let me go through with the wedding — she only needs to hear that I'm engaged, and then she'll come get me and take me back to Stony Landing."

"How can you be sure?"

"Because Mother's had my future planned since I was born. She knows exactly who I will marry and when, and that used to bother me, but it doesn't anymore. And I will tell her that as soon as she arrives." Caroline turned, humming softly to herself, and gazed dreamily out the window. "Mister can think whatever he wants. But once Mother comes to get me, he won't stop her from taking me. And then I'll be home again."

Portia thought Caroline had selected the worst possible moment to develop a sense of conviction. She had never met Caroline's mother, but she knew a thing or two about what happened when someone went far away, how after a time you couldn't see their face anymore when you closed your eyes or hear exactly how they laughed at a joke, how they seemed less like a real person whom you loved and more like a character in a story. And once that happened, it was easy, too easy, to let them float away like milkweed.

Caroline was holding on to her mother. But her mother didn't seem to be doing the same.

Last Letter

Dear Caroline,

Your father and I were quite surprised to receive your news. We never expected that you would find a husband there, but we are as happy as can be, and have told just about everyone we know. We are only disappointed we will not get the chance to witness your marriage firsthand.

We would love to attend, naturally, but as you know summer is a very busy time for us. Perhaps your father and I will come for a visit in the fall. Anyway, I am sure Mr. McGreavey wants to keep you close—you will be a wife now, darling, and your life will be there with your husband. We will, of course, always be your family. But now you must start a family of your own.

With love,
Mother

Little Girl Lost

Portia had brought the letter from town with the rest of the mail—it seemed to weigh more heavily in her hand, to slow her bicycle on the road. She knew Caroline had been waiting to hear from her mother, and she knew, too, that Caroline would not be getting the letter she wanted. She never had.

"I don't understand," Caroline sobbed. "Why don't they want me? I thought they would be proud."

"She says they're happy for you," Portia pointed out.

"But why won't she let me come home?"

"You're getting married. Married women don't live with their parents."

Caroline's shoulders heaved and shuddered like a ship on a stormy sea.

"You really thought she would come for you?" Portia asked softly.

"Of course." Caroline blew her nose into one of the monogrammed handkerchiefs Mister had given her as an early wedding present. Seeing the *M* for *McGreavey* brought fresh tears and even louder sobbing.

"Caroline, please." Portia wanted to help, but she couldn't

abide such weeping. It didn't leave any air in the room for practical thoughts.

"I want to go home," Caroline wailed.

"You can't," Portia said, as gently as she could. Caroline only cried louder. She cried like a heartbroken child, with her whole body and voice. She was making a tremendous amount of noise. Which brought Delilah trotting in to find out what the story was.

Caroline tried to explain, Portia translated Caroline's broken words, and Delilah, as usual, was utterly without sympathy.

"I don't see no problem," she said. "You're gettin' married, you'll have your own money. Whaddaya need your family for? And anyway, they're the ones that sent you here. You're better off without 'em."

Delilah firmly believed that all of the girls at The Home were better off without the families who had callously abandoned them. Even the girls who had been orphaned. Even Lottie Gillaby, whose parents had been struck by lightning during a church revival, an especially unfortunate event after which no one from the church would take Lottie in, having concluded that her family was cursed.

"Delilah, don't you have cleaning to do?" Portia asked.

"Don't *you* have cookin' to do?" Delilah retorted.

"Don't leave me alone!" Caroline wailed. "I don't know what I'll do when I'm alone!"

"You won't be alone for long," Delilah said with a lascivious grin. "There'll be a baby comin' before you know it."

Caroline looked horrified. "There will?"

Portia shook her head. "No, I don't think Mister wants any

kids of his own, not with all of us around already." It seemed a weak argument, and in fact, given Mister's penchant for family history, it was entirely possible that he planned to have a whole herd of children.

But Caroline had grown strangely quiet. She turned to Portia. "You have to help me."

"What can *I* do?"

"You'll think of something," Caroline reassured her, patting her hand with the damp handkerchief. "You're smart. I know you'll think of something."

Portia looked at Caroline, her face patchy with tears and misery, and had the sudden urge to slap her. "I told you not to do this. All along I told you this was a mistake, and you didn't listen to me." She heard her voice rising, a shrill note creeping into its edges, but she could not stop. "If I was so smart, I would have found a way to get myself out of here by now. I wouldn't be stuck here with the rest of you. I wouldn't be cooking and cleaning and working like a slave for *that man*. I would have found my file and I would have found my father and I'd be living in California or wherever the *hell* he is!"

At this, Caroline's face crumpled, and she covered it with her hands. Her sobs pierced Portia like needles, and she was just about to leave the room when Delilah spoke up.

"I know where your file is."

Portia spun around. "What?"

Delilah shrugged, smiled proudly. "Shoulda asked me before."

SOLUTIONS

There were rooms within rooms in Mister's house, and closets within those, and crawlspaces behind those. And somehow Delilah had found the most important door in the entire place. In the entire world, as far as Portia was concerned. A door along the staircase that ran down the back of the house, connecting the upstairs hallway to the kitchen below. A door that led into a narrow, dusty, slant-ceilinged room tucked into the easternmost corner, where Mister kept his best secrets.

Portia wondered later why the door wasn't locked, why Mister hadn't tried harder to protect himself. Perhaps he thought wayward girls weren't so resourceful. Or perhaps he wanted someone to find out what he'd been hiding. Secrets are tricky that way — whatever the cost of revealing them, sometimes the cost of keeping them is even higher.

Portia would find that out for herself, before long.

The burden of knowing this particular secret, the door and the room behind it, had become more than Delilah could bear. She was proud of herself for having found it, Portia could tell, and she was all but hopping up and down as Portia explored the contents of the hidden space.

"Over there." Delilah pointed. "That's where he keeps the files."

The room was so dark that Portia could barely see where Delilah's finger was leading her, but as her eyes adjusted, she made out the sturdy shapes of boxes, and then the dark lines of Mister's jagged handwriting that reminded her of winter branches. L–P 1926, said one. On top of that was D–G 1937.

"Not very organized, is he?" Portia muttered. How long would it take to find the box with the Rs from 1938?

Delilah bumped Portia's shoulder as she wedged herself into the stuffy room. "I left some matches in here somewhere . . . Here they are. Hang on." Portia heard the scuff of a match strike, smelled the burst of sulfur as a bright flame appeared farther to her left than she'd expected. The room was long, traversing the entire length of the house like a hollow backbone.

Delilah held something small and dark in her hand. "What does this say?" she asked. Then she hissed as the match burned down to her fingertips. "Dammit!" Another strike, another tiny light. "C'mere and tell me what this says."

Portia made her way along the colony of boxes and took the object from Delilah. It was a bottle made of brown glass, half full of liquid, with a dry label that was peeling at the edges. There was a skull and crossbones at the corner. STRYCHNINE, it said in faded red letters. POISON. CAUTION. ANTIDOTE: MUSTARD AND WARM WATER TO VOMIT, THEN COLD TEA OR COFFEE, POWDERED CHARCOAL, SEND FOR A PHYSICIAN. J.E.C.F. HARPER & CO., DRUGGISTS. MADISON, IND.

Portia read all of this to Delilah (who had to light two more matches to hear the entire label) without asking why she needed to do so. She had long suspected Delilah couldn't read, ever since she'd found traces of misspelled words in the dirt around the henhouse. MUTHR. FATHR. ILUNOY.

"Wonder what he's got this stashed away for?" Delilah jabbed Portia with her elbow. "Maybe he's got plans to finish us all off, huh?" She did not sound particularly alarmed by this idea.

"It's not just for killing things," Portia told her. "You can use it as medicine. I read about it once. But you have to be careful."

An idea had begun to form in the back corners of her mind.

"You have to be very careful. Use only the smallest amount, and then it doesn't hurt you. Use a little too much, and it makes you sick."

Delilah snorted. "Well, ain't you somethin'? Some kind of doctor, all the sudden?"

"Of course not. I'm only saying, there are other uses for it." Portia slipped the bottle into her dress pocket. They had been here too long—she would return to search the files another time. She pushed past Delilah, retraced her steps toward the door. Then she turned back. "Thank you. For showing me."

Delilah shrugged and ducked her head. "You'd do the same for me, I bet."

"I wish there was something I could do for you," Portia said.

Delilah's head snapped up again. "Bound to be somethin' one a these days," she said. "We'll make us even, sure enough."

"Yes," Portia said. But she was already occupied with another set of thoughts altogether, with how harshly she had spoken to Caroline. How much Caroline needed her help. The bottle in her pocket. So, unwittingly, she made a promise to Delilah.

Sometimes promises are even harder to keep than secrets. Promises are easily made — we toss them like coins bound for a fountain and leave them there, under the water, waiting to be retrieved.

But Delilah never forgot a debt. Especially one that was owed her.

WICKED DEEDS, AND A PLAN

Caroline was skeptical, naturally, but Portia was nothing if not convincing.

"A pinch at a time," Portia told her. "It doesn't taste like anything, and he'll never know it's there."

Caroline frowned. "But it's poison," she said. "It says so right here on the bottle."

Portia patted her knee reassuringly and peeked at the clock on Caroline's nightstand. She had a pocket of time before dinner, and she was eager to get back to the secret room. "Trust me," she said. "It won't kill him. It'll just make him sick, rile up his stomach, give him the jitters maybe. If you can't avoid marrying him, at least you can keep him away from you."

Caroline turned the strychnine over in her hands. "But it *could* kill him, couldn't it? If he took enough of it?"

Portia nodded distractedly. "Yes, of course. But you'll be careful. You won't give him too much." She laughed and patted Caroline's knee again. "You're not a murderer, right?"

"No," Caroline murmured. "Of course not."

WEDDING EVE

Portia was dreaming about a bicycle race—she was miles ahead of the pack when a curious sound started coming from her front wheel. A muffled tapping sound. She slowed down, but the tapping continued, even when she stopped altogether at the side of the road. *They'll be coming soon,* she thought in the dream. *I'll lose my lead.*

Slowly, asleep and awake traded places, and Portia realized that someone was knocking on her bedroom door.

"Who is it?" she whispered.

"Delilah."

"What do you want?"

The knob turned slowly, and the door opened a few inches. Portia could see Delilah's eyes glittering in the dark.

"There's something wrong," Delilah whispered. "It's Caroline."

It was just like a different kind of dream, the way Portia got out of bed and put her bathrobe and slippers on, the way she moved so surely down the hall to the room Caroline had slept in since her woeful engagement, the way she felt she was moving through water and nothing could hurt her.

Until she opened Caroline's door and saw her, twisted like some tortured doll. Gasping for breath. Clutching at the bed sheets as if she were falling like Alice down the rabbit hole.

Delilah stood there, trembling.

"What happened? What's wrong with her?"

And the night voices came back, suddenly, like old friends she had never loved.

You know, they said. *You know exactly what's wrong.*

Delilah just shook her head and took a step toward the door.

"Go get Mister!" Portia hissed, and Delilah ran out.

Portia's thoughts were desperate now, trying to know what to do. She wished she were one of those plucky frontier girls in her dime store novels, a girl who could make a poultice out of a flour sack and some mustard. *Mustard.* She remembered the label on the strychnine bottle. *Mustard and warm water . . . powdered charcoal . . .* But she didn't have those things, didn't know how to use them. There was a glass of water on the nightstand, next to the clock. Portia tried to pour some of the water into Caroline's mouth, but Caroline coughed it out again and knocked the glass from Portia's hand. The sound of it shattering echoed in her ears.

Portia wasn't a nurse. She wasn't the witch on the red bicycle. She had nothing in her head for this.

So she sat on the edge of the bed and held Caroline's hand, rubbed at it to try to straighten the curled fingers. "Shh," she whispered, "shh, it's all right. I'm here. It's all right."

Caroline's eyes were wild, but her body began to calm itself, and she spoke in a ragged whisper. "Mother . . . I'm sorry . . . I couldn't . . ."

"Shh, it's all right."

Delilah came back then, with Mister right behind her. He strolled into the room as if he were calling on a business acquaintance. "What have we here?"

Caroline tried to shield herself with her hands, but she could barely lift them. Her breath shuddered and dragged.

"She needs a doctor," Portia said, as calmly as she could. "She's sick."

Mister ignored her and clucked his tongue at Caroline. "This isn't any way to behave on the eve of your wedding, darling. What would your mother say?"

Just then Caroline began to convulse again, worse than before. Her back arched, her limbs flailed as if they were trying to detach themselves from her body, and her eyes rolled back in her head.

"She's sick!" Portia cried. "She's not *behaving*. Look at her!"

"I can see what she's doing," Mister said, sneering. "And that isn't all I see." He bent down and reached under the bed. His hand came back holding a brown glass bottle. The label had a red bar at the top with a skull and crossbones.

Look, look. The voices hissed and crackled. *Look what you've done.*

"I see someone found Mother's medicine." Still holding the bottle, he leaned over Caroline's thrashing body and murmured, "Naughty girl."

Portia tried to throw herself between them, but Mister grabbed her arm and tossed her to the other side of the room, where Delilah was huddled in the corner, watching Caroline and Mister with huge, unblinking eyes. They stayed there, waiting, watching, as Caroline's back arched and arms and legs grew quiet, as her rasping breath slowed, and then stopped.

"No," Portia pleaded, "no, no! Come back!"

This time Mister did not stop her. She pushed at Caroline's chest where she thought the heart might be, hit it with her fist, shook Caroline's body with all her strength.

But it was not enough.

"I suppose I knew this would happen," Mister said. "She wasn't ready to leave her family, and they weren't ready to take her back. For my part, I wasn't ready to give up their money. Our marriage might have been just the thing for everyone." He turned and, feigning sadness, said, "Alas, our Caroline took matters into her own hands."

Then he grinned and said, "Ah, well. A funeral's just as good as a wedding."

Portia's skin felt like fire. She wanted to kill this man, to see him suffer, burn, bleed to death, anything. He was the one who should have died. Not Caroline.

It's all your fault, the voices said. *You gave her the poison.*

Portia's thoughts fired back. *I told her how to use it. To make Mister sick. To protect herself, not to* kill *herself!*

You should have known she would do this. You put it in her hand. You killed her.

No! Portia's mind was reeling, spinning in weakened circles like a top spun by a child. She wanted to cry out, to make the voices go quiet. But she held her tongue. And the voices kept on.

Murderer, they whispered.

Murderer.

THE FUNERAL

It was dusk, when the processions met.

A train of battered trucks, patched with rust and the wrong colors of paint, limped up the road like a company of wounded soldiers. They were evenly spaced. Some of them towed silver trailers; others hauled only themselves and the people inside, most of whom were concealed by hats or veils or the falling shadows of the trees.

A herd of girls in matching gray dresses, silently marching down the road, followed a single car that had carried Caroline's body to the graveyard. They walked together behind the empty car, each one wondering, *Would I have done the same thing? What if that was me in the box?* For some of them, the thought was not totally unpleasant.

The carnival and the wayward girls eyed one another with naked curiosity. They recognized themselves as compatriots in some foreign country, a country made of many islands, each one so tiny that it held only one person at a time. The carnies and the girls on the road knew exactly what separated them from other people. They knew, at that moment, precisely how much distance was between them.

The last truck in the line looked newer than the rest. It was red. Portia watched as it passed. She couldn't quite see inside because the setting sun cast such a glare on the glass, but there was a thin opening at the top of the passenger-side window, and something flew out of it. It landed in the truck's dusty wake and lay there like a calling card. Portia felt almost too weary to move, but her curiosity gave her just enough energy to bend down and pick the thing up.

It was a thin piece of cardboard with a list of names and numbers printed on it. At the top it said MILLER BROS. CIRCUS.

A memory flashed in her mind, of Max and butter-scented air. Portia slipped the card into her pocket and straightened her shoulders. She watched the red truck as it slid out of sight, stood in the hot, sallow breeze and wished to be a speck in the cloud of dust that followed that slow parade. But she was earthbound. She had never felt so much like stone.

It was only a sharp bark from Mister that compelled her to move. One foot, the other, and so on, until she reached the unwelcoming maw of the house.

Mister gave them the afternoon off. Not all of the girls, of course—the apple trees needed pruning and would not wait for mourning. But Portia and Delilah were granted a respite from their duties, which sent Delilah outdoors in search of skipping rocks and gave Portia a chance to further explore the secret file room. After assuring herself that Mister was properly occupied in his office (aided in his work by a fresh pot of tea and an entire plate of dry biscuits), she made her way upstairs, avoiding the third and seventh steps, which creaked. She looked hard at the floor as she passed Caroline's bedroom. She did not want to remember that now.

Three steps down the back stairs was the door, which had become so familiar to her that Portia knew every nick and imperfection in its face. She opened it carefully, to keep its voice from sounding. She reached to her right, where she had stacked some of the boxes she had already explored, and her fingers caught hold of the small box of matches and the stub of a candle she'd jammed into a discarded beer bottle (collected from the side of the road on her way back from town — Mister indulged in no such habits). She lit the candle and, wetting her finger against her tongue, squeezed the tip of the extinguished match to make sure it was well and truly out. The tiny sting of its hot head between her fingers woke her to her task.

It seemed that no matter how many boxes she looked through, there were more and more beyond, as if the room did not end but stretched itself beyond the edges of the house. In order to keep track of which boxes were done and which had yet to be opened, she had helped herself to one of Mister's green-lined ledgers, in which he recorded his financial gains and losses and other tallies that made less sense to Portia, who was, of course, not their intended audience. In her own stolen pages, she recorded the years and alphabetical designations for each box, as well as certain names that caught her storyteller's heart.

Annika Merrithew

Daisy Sinclair Creamer

Ruby Ledwith

Alice MacEvoy

Evelyn Rose Rossiter

Hazel Danforth

Josephine Ibbotson Tolley

Aside from the constant nagging fear of being discovered, Portia found the work almost soothing. The rhythm of pulling a file from a box, flipping its dusty pages, letting her eyes roam the melee of words typed and scrawled and scratched into paper, letting her mind wander and imagine where these dozens of girls had gone on to.

But there was that urgency, that anxious wondering, that buzzed at the back of her brain all the time. The fear of being caught, and more than that, the fear of not finding her own name on any one of the thousands of pieces of paper hidden in the darkness.

Scraps

The day after the funeral, Portia was ordered to sort through Caroline's belongings.

"She was your friend, after all," Mister said, his voice oily and thick. "You knew her better than anyone."

There was a condemnation wrapped inside the words, a reprimand. Again Portia heard them: *You should have known she would do this. You should have stopped her. Saved her.*

Mister leaned in. "If you find anything . . . that might further grieve her family . . . bring it to me."

Portia didn't imagine she'd find anything that could be worse for Caroline's family than the fact that the girl had poisoned herself—and if she did, she would never turn it over to Mister. But she nodded and went upstairs.

The room still smelled like Caroline, like the rose-scented soap she used, the only comfort her mother had ever sent aside from her letters (which weren't, in the end, very comforting at all). Portia closed her eyes and imagined that when she opened them again, Caroline would be there, in her bed, pale and alive.

Portia, she would say, *I'm feeling better now. Let's go for a walk in the orchard.* And they would put on their sweaters because the orchard was chilly at night, and they would link their arms together, and Portia would let Caroline talk about the parties at home, listen as she described her dresses in excruciating detail, and never call her silly.

But even as she opened her eyes, she knew it would not be true. There was only the empty bed, which Delilah had made up with fresh sheets as soon as the body had been taken, and the empty room, and the silence. A few plain cotton dresses in the closet, a nightgown and some underthings in the dresser, a yellow sweater, a cream one — Portia folded everything neatly and put it in Caroline's blue suitcase. Her mother might send for it.

There was a small stack of books on the nightstand, wholesome stories that had been donated to The Home by local church ladies. Stories of redemption for the inspiration of wayward girls. Portia preferred the books in Mister's library, wholly inappropriate for young ladies, but Caroline hadn't been willing to risk getting caught where she didn't belong and so she'd settled for the church ladies' choices.

Portia put the books in the suitcase as well, just in case it was requested by Caroline's family. *At least her mother will see she was trying to be good,* she thought. *Might help, somehow.* Though, if she was being honest, she didn't feel much like Caroline's mother deserved to feel better.

Not if Portia had to feel so bad.

She looked around the room again, totally empty now, and was about to shut the suitcase when her eyes settled on the nightstand drawer. Almost as if someone else were lifting her arm, her hand went to the handle and pulled it open.

It was filled with torn paper.

Torn paper like strips of birch bark, with black writing on every piece.

The letters.

Caroline had shredded them, every one from her mother, laid them in the drawer like a bird's nest. Her last act of defiance.

Good girl, Portia thought. And then she gathered the paper scraps into her arms, sat down on the bed, and wept hot, bitter tears.

When she was finished — for she allowed herself only a few minutes of such behavior at a time — she gathered the shreds of the letters and laid them gently in the suitcase, spread them across Caroline's clothes, tucked them into each corner. Then her eyes caught sight of her own name, written by this stranger's hand, and she had the sudden urge to seize it. As she folded the lone piece of soft white paper into her pocket, her fingers touched something stiff. She pulled it out.

It was the slip of cardboard from the red truck.

She looked more closely now. Down the left-hand side of the card, there was a list of names. Towns, she realized. Not Brewster Falls, of course, but others that were not far away. Next to the towns there were numbers — dates and distances.

It was the circus's schedule for the summer, the map of their route. They had come from Jacksonville and were headed for Winchester, which was only a few miles away.

The first line said MAY 14 — BURLINGTON — 20 MILES — U.S. 61.

My birthday, she thought. Just over a week ago. She hadn't even known it *was* her birthday until she'd accidentally seen the date on Mister's newspaper, folded neatly on his desk. Portia wondered if there was a girl in Burlington who had turned fourteen that day, if she had gone to the circus to celebrate.

Something began to move in Portia's memory, reluctant as a rusted wheel—the old story she had made for herself, in which Max had run off with the circus. How many circuses were there? Fewer, Portia knew, than there had been before. Movie theaters and dancehalls cropped up like pretty weeds, common and alluring, and without the strange elements that came with traveling shows. Mister had frequently lectured her on the topic of such distasteful forms of entertainment.

But Max loved a good time. And a circus was certainly that. Even if he wasn't still with *this* circus, someone might have seen him, known him, heard about his beloved daughter.

Only a few miles away, Portia thought.

Even by bicycle.

One Last Chance

Once the idea of Max and the circus solidified in her head, Portia allowed herself to spend a small part of each day speculating about her future — when she would leave and how, where she would go, what she might find there — but she was careful not to overindulge. Mister had a kind of radar for these things, and she could not afford to have him sniff her out. She went on teaching Delilah how to cook, despite Delilah's objections that she "didn't need to know none of this kind of thing," as she was going to be an actress someday and would never ever cook for herself or anyone else.

"But what if," Portia said, "you need to play the part of a cook on stage?"

Delilah considered this and grudgingly agreed that it might be useful to know a few things, just for appearances.

"Nothing fancy, though," she insisted. "I don't want no one mistaking me for a servant."

Portia refrained from pointing out that unless Delilah started speaking like a lady, she would surely never be mistaken for that instead. "Of course not," she said. "We'll stick to the basics. Get the eggs."

Tempting as it was to request another girl to help with the housework (since Delilah was generally preoccupied with observing herself in any and all reflective surfaces), Portia resisted for two reasons: she loathed the idea of asking Mister for any kind of favor, and she did not want to have to account for the whereabouts of another person in the house every time she crept into the secret room to search for her file. Between the cooking, the cleaning, the trips into town, and these covert missions, Portia was utterly exhausted by the end of the day and frequently slept so deeply that she could not muster any kind of dream onto the blank screen behind her eyelids.

But every night, just for a moment, she made herself remember when she was five, the air carrying stories from the garden, Max's good-night kisses, the tail of his truck fading in the dust. She made sure that this room she had been given would never feel like home. She wouldn't let it.

The list of names in her notebook grew longer, and the number of boxes she had yet to search through steadily waned. Still, she found no mention of Max, her family, anyone she knew, anyone who might care to find her or be found. She wondered if Sophia felt guilty for leaving her behind, then pushed the thought roughly away. She bowed her head, continued reading, writing down the names, recording the history of the man who she vowed would not keep her much longer.

It was a Tuesday.

It was raining.

Portia was dusting the downstairs hallway when Mister opened the study door. But he did not walk through it. He simply looked at Portia, unsurprised, as if he'd expected to see her exactly where she was, and then he crooked his finger like a fishhook and reeled her in.

"Portia," he said, "may I see you for a moment?"

It was a rhetorical question. She was already walking to him.

He sat down behind his desk and gestured to the chair opposite him. "Close the door," he said, "and have a seat."

Mister's speech, always, was clipped as neat as whiskers, and his voice did not waver. Never in anger, certainly never in grief. Portia thought of the Tin Man and how he rusted himself with tears. Mister's metal was far tougher than that.

She sat perfectly still. She did not want to disturb anything, did not want to leave her impression in this place. It had bothered her, before, to think that she could simply disappear. Now it seemed necessary, the perfect first step of her escape.

"Portia."

She hated to hear him say her name, but still, she didn't move.

"I know you must be terribly"—he folded his hands on his desk, leaned forward—"sad. About Caroline."

Was that all he expected? Sadness? What about guilt? The heart-wrenching weight of responsibility? She had brought Caroline here, had led her straight to the lion's mouth and watched the horrible jaws close around Caroline's hopeful face. Perhaps he did not know it had been Portia's idea to move out of the bunkhouse. Perhaps Caroline had never told him.

"Yes, sir," Portia said, primly as she could. She would not let her voice waver, either, even if it meant actually gripping her throat with her hand.

"It is difficult, isn't it, to imagine that she's gone," he went on. "Poor girl. Taken from us so suddenly. I think she scarcely recognized me, at the end. Calling for her mother until the very last breath she took."

As if Portia did not know. As if she had not been there, listening to that last breath.

As if she could not hear it still.

"Yes, it's very sad." Mister sighed. "But we must move on, mustn't we?"

Oh, his voice was smooth, oily as warm butter.

"I don't mind telling you, Portia, that I have achieved some measure of success with my . . . enterprises. The orchards are thriving, and now that our army seems to be mobilizing for action in Europe, I expect the need for uniforms will be greater than ever."

Portia imagined an army of carefully hemmed trousers, marching across the nations of the world, and had to swallow a laugh.

"I want to speak with you, Portia, about *your* future."

He stood up then and walked halfway around the desk, sat on the corner, and crossed his legs so one knee was dangerously close to Portia's. And went on talking as if he had not moved.

"You get on very well with the other girls, don't you? Telling them stories and jokes and such? Keeping their morale up?"

So Caroline had told him a few things.

"You are an intelligent girl, Portia. One might even say an *unusual* girl."

She watched the space between them, saw its borders shrink a bit more.

"You are not the kind of girl to let an opportunity pass you by. Am I correct?"

"That depends, sir," she replied, "on the conditions of the prospect."

Mister smiled, curling his lips carefully, as if he were imitating something he'd seen in a picture.

"Fair enough," he said, and leaned a little closer. "I would like for you to be my assistant."

"Like Caroline was?" She did not mean to sound snide. It was, mostly, a question of fact.

"Not precisely," he said. "I have no interest, for instance, in marrying you. I don't believe I'll make that mistake again."

Portia fought the ripple of revulsion that crawled up her spine.

"I will employ you to manage my work force and organize my accounts, for which I will provide you a salary."

What sort of buffoon considers a bunch of rejected girls a work force? Portia thought.

"Furthermore," Mister purred, "you will report to me on the . . . shall we say, conduct of the young ladies, and bring any insolence, rebellion, or idleness to my attention immediately."

"You want me to be a rat," Portia said. "Pardon my language."

"Does that offend you?" Mister asked.

"Not necessarily," she said. "But I might require some further compensation."

"Such as?"

"I want my file."

He drew back. "Portia," he said, voice low and wary, "I'm not sure what you mean."

"My file," she said, matching his tone. "I want it."

It was not a request she expected he would grant. She was not asking for a favor. She felt she could afford to reveal that she knew a secret and was not afraid to speak of it. It was a gambit, a tip of her hand. After she was gone, he would know that he had not controlled her.

Mister stood up then and returned to the other side of his desk, sinking into his chair with an almost imperceptible smile.

"I understand the importance of one's family history." He waved one hand stiffly toward the wall of books next to him, without breaking Portia's gaze. "This entire house, after all, is my family legacy. Where would I be without it? Where would any of us be?"

A whole lot happier, Portia was tempted to say.

"But understand," Mister said, "that it is at my discretion to tell you what you need to know about your family. You must trust me, Portia. Haven't I treated you well?"

"Better than you treated Caroline, maybe."

Mister shrugged. "Caroline was a troubled girl," he said, "and I do feel badly about the way things . . . turned out. But that proves my point, don't you see? She wrote to her mother about our marriage without telling me, and she suffered because of it. Had she only asked, I would have told her to wait. I would have found the right time, and we could have avoided the entire mess."

Portia remembered trying to straighten Caroline's twisted, bloated fingers and nearly gagged.

"I'm not Caroline," she said. "And I deserve to know where my father is."

"Don't you mean, where your *parents* are?"

"I mean what I mean," Portia replied. She had long since absolved herself of any guilt she felt whenever she thought only of Max. Her mother had simply melted into the landscape like the ghost she had always been.

"Regardless of semantics," Mister said, sneering, "what is the point of this pursuit? They don't care to know anything about who you are or what you want. They left you here, my girl, and they are not coming back for you. Surely you know that by now."

"You're wrong." Portia forced the words past the tremendous weight she felt in her chest, her throat, everywhere. "My family is looking for me."

"But Portia," Mister replied, his voice false and sweet, "*I* am your family now."

It was then Portia knew that she was right to leave, because if Mister found a way to claim her, she would never get away. She would spend the rest of her life in this limbo state, floating invisibly through Mister's haunted hallways. And worse than becoming one of Mister's possessions, worse than spending the rest of her days as a wayward girl, Portia knew that if she stayed, eventually Mister's words would tunnel through her skin and enter her veins like a virus. She would come to believe him.

She would give up.

Portia stood—carefully, as if she might shatter by moving too quickly—and made her way to the door. Mister did not stop her. There was nothing more to say, after all. He had led Portia to a grim realization that, he expected, would tamp out the last flicker of hope she carried. As he had done for Caroline. For so many girls.

Hope, Mister believed, was a waste of time. And it made girls so terribly willful.

He felt he could almost see through Portia now, see the hope draining out of her like water through a sieve. It thrilled him from top to toes. He could barely keep himself from clapping.

ESCAPE

It had been drizzling all day, and there was still all that water in the air that couldn't quite make itself into rain. It caught on Portia's coat and her hair as she moved through it. It stowed away.

Caroline's blue suitcase was strapped on the back of the bicycle. Portia had kidnapped Caroline's belongings, knowing that they would likely never be retrieved by her neglectful mother but would instead be relegated to the collection of discarded items left by other girls over the years. She could not stand to think of Caroline's things in that trunk, gathering dust and the hazy scent of mildew. From underneath the blanket of torn letters, she had carefully extracted the good-girl books (repellent things) and pushed them underneath the dresser in her room. Her own clothes remained in its drawers. This was her exodus, her new beginning, and it seemed fitting for her to take whatever she could of Caroline along.

Perhaps, Portia thought, it might count as a kind of penance. She hoped it would not be considered grand larceny instead.

She had her little cloth bag in the bicycle's basket, with some stolen food, her stolen ledger, and Caroline's letter scraps. She wasn't going to leave them with Mister. He didn't deserve to keep them. Even if he didn't know he had them.

She had a trowel from the garden shed.

She had a stop to make before she left town.

She was leaving later than she had wanted to because Mister, usually a creature of habit, had changed his evening routine and demanded coffee in the parlor before he went upstairs to bed. Portia stood in the hall and waited, watched the minutes shudder past while he sipped from his mother's best china cup and set it into its matching saucer. *Sip. Clink. Sip. Clink.*

It was maddening.

Finally, he set cup and saucer on the tray next to his chair and waved his hand once, signaling Portia to retrieve everything and take it to the kitchen. She left the dishes in the sink. By the time Delilah got up in the morning, Portia thought, she'd be miles away and out of earshot. Delilah could yell all she wanted about having to do Portia's work.

When she walked back down the hallway and peeked into the parlor, Mister was gone. She hadn't heard his feet on the stairs, but that wasn't unusual. The house had a way of swallowing sound, turning its inhabitants into silent apparitions. Portia looked around at the dark wood walls, at the worn floors, at the stairs that sagged in the middle. She knew every squeaky spot, every knot in the wood, every dull patch where the finish had worn off under years of thoughtless assault by feet and hands. She was surprised to find herself feeling a twinge of something — regret? longing? — as she readied herself to leave.

But there was no time for that.

She ducked down the hall to the kitchen, where she had hidden her belongings under the sink earlier that morning.

She made her way to the back door, opened it carefully so it wouldn't cry out and betray her, and slipped into darkness. Down the steps. Around the corner of the house. The bicycle was waiting.

It was all so simple.

Except for this:

As Portia pushed off and began to pedal, as the gravel crunched under her wheels and she felt the first rush of motion toward her freedom, one lone shaft of moonlight touched her path and revealed her, just for a moment. And Delilah, watching from the upstairs window, saw her go.

Something about a place where no one has ever been happy makes you pedal extra hard to get away.

Because of the fog and because the shadows were deep, Portia had to feel her way into the cemetery, along the stone wall, to find the gate, down the gate to find the latch. It lifted easily. This gate, unlike others in town, was never locked. Maybe because it was like an extension of the church and God's door was always supposed to be open. Not a door Portia had ever knocked on before, but for Caroline, she made an exception.

She could see just well enough to find the outline of Mister's family mausoleum, where generations of ill will were buried. Caroline's grave was behind it, under a plain slab with a plain engraving Portia traced with her index finger.

CAROLINE ELIZABETH SALES
JANUARY 10, 1922 – MAY 22, 1939
RESIDENT OF THE MCGREAVEY HOME

It had always been easy for Portia to forget that Caroline was three years older — she had been so fragile, so quick to shatter. But seeing the numbers etched in stone, Portia could not help but think how quickly she would surpass Caroline's final age.

The last line, in smaller type than the rest, was the evidence of Mister's concession to bury Caroline among his family members. He had, of course, refused her admission into the mausoleum itself but agreed to house her on the McGreavey plot. Caroline's family had requested this, for they did not want their own land sullied by suicide.

Portia wished for a sharper tool, something that could scratch Mister's wretched name off Caroline's grave so she wouldn't have to spend eternity pinned underneath it. But there was only the trowel.

And she could not afford to spend the time, precious currency that it was.

Portia began to dig. The dirt was still loose at the base of Caroline's headstone, and it was quick work to fashion a pocket in the ground just large enough to hold the collection of letters that Caroline had torn so thoroughly apart. Portia couldn't have said why, exactly, she felt that this was the correct place for them. It was entirely possible that Caroline would be angered by this and come back from the Great Beyond to nag Portia unceasingly.

Portia almost hoped that she would.

Perhaps she was simply tempting fate.

Her task completed, she patted the soil back into place, tucking in a few errant strands of paper that peeked out of the dirt like curious insects. She decided against taking the trowel with her and looked around for a good spot in which to leave it. It was only then that she noticed the other headstones.

Twenty or thirty of them, set even farther behind the mausoleum than Caroline's lone monument. They were arranged in two long rows, like chess pieces. Portia pulled her coat more tightly around herself and stepped closer, close enough to read a name.

RUBY LEDWITH

The cold she felt now was nothing to do with the rain, or the graveyard air. She peered at the marker next to Ruby's.

DAISY SINCLAIR CREAMER

And the next.

HAZEL DANFORTH

There were names that were new to her as well, but most of them were familiar. She did not need to check her notebook; she had read the names so many times that she knew them as well as if she had known the girls themselves. As if they all had been friends once, instead of just coincidental passengers on the same nightmarish vessel. And here they were, her imaginary friends.

She had wondered, hadn't she, what had become of them?

Now she knew. Mister was worse than what even she had imagined. He had recognized something in her, she thought, after Caroline died. Another killer. A kindred spirit.

She sat down, hard, on the damp grass.

She sat there for a long time.

Portia could not see Mister's house from where she sat, but she felt it there, gazing down at her from the hill, sending its dank breath through the fog to surround her. Finally, shaking, unsteady, she made her way back to the bicycle, took her place on its back, and began to move.

PART TWO

WELCOME TO THE WONDER SHOW

Portia's legs ached, but she kept pedaling. Her toes were numb, and her feet were burning and swollen in her shoes, but she kept pedaling. She kept going until she found the circus.

The rain had finally stopped and her clothes were nearly dry, but parts of the road were too muddy for riding, and she had to walk the last mile. She kept her eyes forward, trying not to think about the small army of headstones in the graveyard, the girls pinned beneath them like butterflies under glass. When she saw the tips of the huge tents piercing the dawn-streaked sky, she almost wept with relief. Before she arrived at the foot of those canvas peaks, however, she found herself surrounded by a smaller cluster of trucks, trailers, and tents that were dwarfed by the rest.

There was a boy sitting in the back of a pickup truck, shaggy-haired and lanky, his face pink with sun. He was reading as if the whole world around him were nothing more than a painting. But he looked up when Portia stopped in front of him, and she just started talking, before she lost her nerve.

"You work here?" She tried to keep her voice even, but she

was breathing hard, and she had to squint because the sun was behind him.

"Yes," he said.

"Are you the boss?"

"Only of myself."

"Well, is there a boss for everyone else?" She was getting a headache behind her eyes, and her shoes, still damp, rubbed at the edges of her feet. "Someone I can talk to about a job?"

"That'd be Mosco," he said.

The boy folded the page corner down, closed his book, and climbed out of the truck. Closer up, he looked older than Portia had thought. And taller, too. She had seen young men on her trips into Brewster Falls, but those boys had seemed like paintings, part of the scenery, separated from her by great expanses. They met her eye only occasionally, by accident, and they never exchanged words or held her gaze. This boy did. Embarrassed that he might think she was staring, Portia diverted her eyes to the truck and saw that it was red.

"Is this your truck?" she asked.

"It's the truck I drive." He grinned and pointed at the red bicycle. "Your favorite color?"

She wanted to ask about the slip of cardboard, the one with the dates and towns that had seemed so much like a secret message meant just for her. But she knew it would sound strange, possibly even crazy, so she asked instead, "Can you take me to Mosco?"

Neither of them spoke as they wove between the fading painted trailers, ducked under half-empty clotheslines, passed through the temporary town the circus became when it was settled in place. It seemed so familiar, this progression of shapes and structures, like the set of a play Portia had seen before. She kept both hands on her bicycle, leading it beside her as if it were a dog that might try to run away. When they came to the midway, Portia saw a bigger cluster of trucks and trailers on the other side, like a small city, and heard the strange calls of animals through the heavy air. Brawny roustabouts roamed the slim spaces between everything else, hoisting coils of rope, bales of hay, equipment, toting all of these things like ants carrying crumbs to their colony.

"That's the circus," the boy told her. "You want a circus job, gotta talk to the ringmaster. You want a carnival job, you talk to Mosco."

She wasn't about to admit she didn't know the difference. "Lead the way," she said.

Mosco turned out to be a squat, bulky man with the most perfectly bald head Portia had ever seen. He was holding a huge iron ball in both hands, curling it toward his chest and back out again. The muscles in his arms looked like the ropes that staked the tents to the ground. He looked, Portia thought, like a man made of fists.

The boy cleared his throat, and Mosco dropped the iron ball on the ground with a satisfying thud. He put his cap on and said, "Gideon."

Portia realized then that she hadn't known the boy's name or told him hers. She still had the chance to make up a new identity for herself, a fake name, a tragic story. But she was unnerved when Mosco suddenly removed his hat again to wipe his forehead. The sun shone off his bald head like a spotlight, and when he growled, "Who're you?" she blurted, "Portia Remini, sir."

"Whaddya want?"

Gideon cut in. "She wants a job. Maybe she could help in the pie car."

"What is she, your girlfriend or something?"

Gideon blushed violently. Portia fought the urge to laugh.

"I can make pies," she said. "Apple, cherry, whatever you want."

"Pie car's not for making pie," Mosco grumbled. "Ain't even a car since we went back to being a truck show."

"The pie car's the kitchen," Gideon explained.

"I can cook. Just about anything. My Aunt Sophia taught me all her recipes . . ." She could hear the desperation in her own voice, and it made her feel itchy.

Mosco grunted. "Can you make chicken-fried steak?"

"Of course," she said. "Best you've ever had."

He put his cap on again.

"You're hired," he said. "For now. But I want chicken-fried steak for dinner tonight, and if it's no good, we're leaving you here when we pull up stakes."

"Fair enough," Portia said.

"She can stay with Violet," Mosco told Gideon. "Waste of space, that girl having a trailer all to herself."

"Right," said Gideon.

As they walked away, he asked, "Is your chicken-fried steak really that good?"

Portia shrugged. "Don't know. I've never made it before."

"Oh."

"How hard can it be?" Portia heard the faintest note of fear in her voice. She hoped Gideon hadn't detected it.

"Right," he said again. Then, nodding at the red bicycle, "Can I take that for you?"

She was surprised to find that she did not want to hand it over. Her grip tightened on the handlebars, and she stopped walking. "Maybe you could show me a safe place. Where I could keep it."

He nodded, paused. Waited until she moved again. He did not rush her.

Violet Lucasie did not look like a carny.

She looked, in fact, like many of the girls from The Home — she wore an expression that was a mixture of hope and weariness, that said she was waiting for something better to come along but wasn't holding her breath.

Portia knew that look, and she was almost relieved to see it. It meant that maybe she was not in a completely foreign place after all.

Violet was sitting in a beach chair outside a trailer with chipped wood paneling, wearing huge sunglasses that were, Portia supposed, meant to look glamorous. She was reading a movie magazine and teasing one molasses-black curl with her index finger.

Gideon cleared his throat. "Hey, Violet."

"Hey yourself," said Violet, still looking at her magazine.

"I brought you something," Gideon said.

Portia wasn't fond of being referred to as "something," but for all she knew, this was common custom in the carnival world. She hid her annoyance and extended her hand. "Portia."

Violet rolled her eyes up slowly and looked at Portia over her sunglasses. Portia's hand stayed up, and after a long minute Violet reached out and shook it.

"You staying with me?"

"Guess so."

"Mosco said," Gideon added.

"Fine by me," said Violet. "It'll be nice to have another *normal* around." She bit into the word like it was a tough piece of meat.

Gideon didn't take the bait. "You'll bring her to the pie car later on?"

"Sure. She can help me with the dinner shift."

Gideon nodded, tipped an invisible hat to Portia, and walked off toward the midway.

"What's a 'normal'?" Portia asked, as soon as he was out of earshot.

"I am," Violet said. "And Gideon. And you, unless you're hiding something." She winked.

Portia said nothing.

"Don't you know where you are?" Violet asked her.

"Youngsville?"

"God only knows. I don't mean the town." Violet twirled a finger at the trailers, the dead-grass midway, the tents, the thick smells, everything. "I mean *this*."

"The carnival?"

"This is no ordinary carnival, darling. You've signed on with Mosco's Traveling Wonder Show."

Portia still felt itchy and hot. "Sounds fine to me."

Violet smirked. "Then clearly you've never been through the ten-in-one." She cupped her hands around her mouth and hollered, "Step right up! Behold the terrible wonders of nature! The Fattest Woman in the World! The Lobster Boy! The Dreaded Albinos of Darkest Africa!"

Portia's sleeping memory stirred again, revealing a stage, the view from a stranger's shoulders as she watched The Pinhead playing the accordion. The man in the white suit. The sign that said STRANGE PEOPLE. She remembered Aunt Sophia's hand pulling her away. *It's not appropriate.*

Violet stood up and stepped close so her mouth was almost touching Portia's ear. "Welcome to the freak show, little girl."

And despite the heat in the air all around her, Portia shivered.

The Pie Car

Violet never stopped talking. She talked while Portia un-
packed (which wasn't really unpacking because she had so little and also because she didn't want to get too settled, in case
Mosco left her behind after the chicken-fried steak test). She
talked through the trailer door while Portia changed into her
other dress, the one that wasn't covered with dust and sweat
from riding a bicycle across the prairie. She talked all the way
from the trailer to the pie car and kept talking while she and
Portia sliced a crateful of carrots and another of potatoes. They
all went into the biggest pot of boiling water Portia had ever
seen—or perhaps it seemed big only because the kitchen was
so small. It was in a converted trailer, which, like all the other
trailers that belonged to the carnival, was about half the size
of a school bus. The inside had all sorts of shelves and cabi-
nets that fit together like a jigsaw puzzle, and the aisle down
the middle was just wide enough for Portia to stand back to
back with Violet, which meant she could pretend to be listening and didn't have to nod or make eye contact to keep up the
charade.

"Mosco contracts with small-time circuses, shows with trick

riders and dog acts and a tightrope walker or two. Maybe they have a menagerie with a few old elephants and patchy tigers. This season's show is better than most—the troupe of clowns has a first-rate act going. But you'll never see them on the midway."

"Why not?" asked Portia.

"It's because of Mosco. He hates clowns. His wife left him for Greggo the Great," Violet said. "He's this famous clown that dresses like a magician and does tricks that go all wrong. Like he goes to pull a rabbit out of his hat, and the rabbit hops out from behind him instead. People can't get enough, for some reason."

"So clowns make Mosco . . . upset?"

"Mosco sees a clown, he goes berserk," Violet said. "'Specially one that looks like Greggo. I've seen him come near to taking a man's head off 'cause he showed up in a top hat."

"So they all know to stay away?"

"They know. He's famous for it. Plus he puts it in the contract with the circus."

Violet knew all about Mosco's arrangements because she worked in the office for him. She said it was tedious work but far better than talking on the bally or serving in the meal tent. There wasn't much for normal girls to do on the lot.

"Huh," said Portia.

Violet kept talking, and Portia kept thinking. About Caroline. About Delilah, left behind in Mister's house. About Mister and what his face might have looked like when he found out she was gone. About whether he would try to get her back, or whether he would let her go.

More than one girl had tried to run away since Portia had

been living there. Every single one got brought back, one way or another.

Not me, Portia thought. The carnival was a good place to hide out, seemed like, and she needed to stay only long enough to find out if Max was here or if anyone knew him. There was just one thing she needed to do to buy herself that time.

"Hey, Violet?"

"Yeah."

"Do you know how to make chicken-fried steak?"

There was a pause in the sound of Violet's knife, and then it picked up again. "Nope. But Doula might. She's got a bunch of old cookbooks in her trailer, and I think they're mostly Russian or something, but maybe there's one or two that're in English. She'd probably let you look at them."

"Who's Doula?"

"She's the gypsy fortuneteller, y'know, with the crystal ball and everything. She tells futures for a dollar. Two dollars if you want to know how you're going to die." Violet laughed. "Apparently I'm going to live to a ripe old age and die in my sleep. If you believe what Doula's got to say about it."

"Do you?"

"Believe her? Not really. I mean, she's been right about some things, like last year one of the tigers got out of its cage and almost killed a trainer, and Doula knew about it two or three weeks beforehand. But it's a circus, y'know? Stuff like that always happens."

Portia hadn't considered the possibility of getting mauled by a tiger. Maybe she should pay the two dollars to make sure that wasn't how she'd be passing to the next world.

"Anyway," Violet said, "she's a nice old lady. A little weird, usually a little drunk. But she's nice. We'll see her at breakfast — I'll ask her if we can stop by later."

When the potatoes and carrots were sufficiently boiled, Violet wrapped her hands with dishtowels and hoisted the huge pot off the stove and emptied the whole thing straight into the sink. She waited until the water had drained and then picked up handfuls of vegetables, threw them back into the pot, unwrapped her hands, and said, "Breakfast is served. Or is it lunch? Hard to keep track when you've been on the road all night."

"That's it?" Portia asked.

"Pretty much," Violet said. "There's some cold chicken in the refrigerator. We'll throw that on a plate, too. Nothing fancy. We eat better, sometimes, when we're closer to town and we can . . . er . . . borrow from people's gardens."

"You have to steal food?"

"Not always. But money's not coming in like it used to. And fresh-grown tastes better than store-bought, anyway." Violet smiled. "Especially when it's free."

"Have you ever gotten caught?"

Violet shrugged. "Once or twice. Mosco or Jackal can usually talk us out of trouble, though. Give the rubes some free tickets and a special tour, they forget about their missing turnips pretty fast. Especially after they see the freaks."

The thing Violet had said about having another "normal" around was still buzzing around Portia's brain. So far she hadn't seen anyone but Gideon and Mosco, and they looked plenty normal to her. She recalled the odd man playing the accordion, The Pinhead—he had been quite irregular, and she hadn't been bothered by him, even though she was only a child then.

She had heard about so-called human curiosities, seen pictures in the magazines Mister arranged in perfect stacks on his desk, but she was not prepared for them to appear as they did. As real as she was.

They seemed to come out of the ground itself, moving silently toward the meal tent, where the picnic tables and benches waited like an empty church. A tribe of misfits. Portia wanted to look away, to run, to make them stand still, but she could only watch as they drew closer. She could only try, desperately, to make sense of what she was seeing.

A man tall as a tree, bent at the waist like a sapling, curling over a child-size man who walked in front of him with stiff, hopping steps.

An enormous, sweating creature in a massive calico dress, rolling to the tent like a wave of flesh and fabric.

Two girls in one silk dress, arms wrapped around each other, manicured hands resting gently on smooth white shoulders.

A slim, delicate woman whose face was covered with dark, wiry hair.

A girl with no arms.

Just when Portia had begun to feel that the ground was solid under her feet, the world seemed to tip and slide once more. Her night in the graveyard, her bicycle flight, her sudden immersion in the sideshow—they all crashed together like an avalanche, and Portia could not hold them back any longer.

She fainted.

PRACTICAL MATTERS

Doula's face was a fierce collection of deep creases and steep bones under her papery skin. Her nose was straight from the front, but when she turned to the side, she had a profile like a woman on an ancient coin. The skin under her chin gathered like pleated fabric and swayed when she spoke.

"You got money?"

Violet swiftly grabbed Portia's hand and held it up as if it were a prize she'd found on the midway. "This is Portia," she said. "She's working with me in the pie car." Violet made no mention of Portia's humiliating fainting episode. Everyone, it seemed, had seen such reactions before.

"Congratulations. You want a prize or something?"

Doula's voice was gravelly and very deep. Portia would have thought she was a man, if she could only hear the voice and not see the impressive display of cleavage below Doula's craggy face. The rest of her body was swathed in yards of dark silk, enough to conceal whatever form was underneath, and in the dim light it seemed that Doula was, in fact, a disembodied head. With cleavage.

Violet rolled her eyes. "No, thank you. Portia's got to make dinner tonight, and it's got to be good or Mosco's leaving her here. Can we look at your cookbooks?"

Doula stepped back just enough to let them in.

Her trailer was packed with things: piles of dusty books, half-dead plants in cracked ceramic pots, silver spoons, scarves and strings of beads hanging from open drawers, shoeboxes full of playing cards, rows of hand-size dolls peering out of the darkness with their glassy eyes. Every flat surface was covered with objects, so it seemed as though there actually were no flat surfaces at all, just a landscape of mismatched belongings.

"Cookbooks are over there," Doula said, waving a limp hand in the general direction of the back of her home. "I stay outside."

"She doesn't like to be in small spaces with anyone else," Violet explained. "She says it's bad for her aura to absorb too much energy from other people."

Portia stumbled over something with blunt edges and scraped her shin.

"Careful," Violet said. "God only knows what she's got hidden in here."

"Probably not even God," said Portia.

"Probably not. I don't think Doula would let him in."

Doula's cookbooks turned out to be no help at all, being mostly compendiums of recipes for Greek delicacies that involved ingredients Portia would never be able to find (or want to handle, even if she had them).

"What are you going to do?" asked Violet. "Mosco said—"

"I'll just have to improvise," Portia replied.

She strode back to the pie car as fast as she could, hoping that Violet would fall behind so she'd have time to think. But Violet was a fast walker.

"How're you gonna do that?"

Portia shrugged. "Make something that tastes good and tell a good story about it. Most people will eat what you give them."

"Mosco isn't most people."

"No one is," Portia replied.

"Especially not around here," Violet said.

Portia looked up. There was a cloud shaped like her apple tree. "Not anywhere," she said.

The Chicken-Fried Steak Trial

This doesn't look like chicken-fried steak to me," Mosco said.

"That's because it's not," said Portia.

"Deal was you make chicken-fried steak and you get to stay. *Good* chicken-fried steak."

"That's true," said Portia.

"So what are you trying to pull?"

"Well, sir, my Aunt Sophia was the greatest chef ever to leave the coast of Italy for the shores of America. All she brought to this great land was a recipe book and a pocket full of basil, and when she arrived at Ellis Island, she asked the guard, she said, 'Escuse me, sir, but where will I find best Italian cooking in city?' And the guard told her where to go, and she went, and that very day they hired her to cook for them." Portia leaned in. "And this is what she made for them."

Mosco looked at his plate. "You expect me to believe that the best Italian restaurant in New York hired your aunt because she made macaroni with meat sauce?"

Portia put her hands on her hips and tried to look outraged and good-natured at once. "That's *pasta con la salsa della carne!"* Of course, Aunt Sophia would have been aghast to hear Portia crediting her for this dish. After searching the pie car unsuccessfully for anything resembling pasta or tomatoes, Violet had suggested sending Gideon into town for a case of canned spaghetti, which was paid for from Portia's meager and precious savings.

"Which means what?" asked Mosco.

"Which means," said a man as he sidled up to the table, "pasta with meat sauce. Subtle difference."

He wore suspenders over his undershirt and dust from the cuffs of his pants to the brim of his bowler hat. Even his arms were coated with dust. Only his face was clean, and maybe his hands, which Portia couldn't see because they were in his pockets. He was leaning against one of the tent poles and chewing on an unlit cigar.

"Didn't know you spoke Italian, Jackal," Mosco said.

"I'm willing to wager there's a great deal you don't know about me, dear fellow." Jackal stood up straight and stepped to the table. "Aren't you going to eat your dinner?"

"This isn't my dinner. I asked for chicken-fried steak, and this one" — Mosco waved his fork at Portia — "is trying to back out of the deal."

"Is that true?" Jackal asked her.

"No, sir," she said. "I'm simply offering him something better."

"Well, then, the next step seems obvious. Mosco?"

"Agh," Mosco grunted. He dug his fork into the pile of broken noodles and oversweet tomato sauce and grudgingly shoved it into his mouth. Chewed. Chewed some more. Swallowed. Looked at Portia and said, "That's pretty good."

Sometimes a small victory is the best kind. And sometimes it's simply short-lived.

"But it ain't chicken-fried steak. And a deal's a deal. We leave tomorrow. Without you."

Portia's head began to itch. "Please, give me another chance. I can't—"

"No second chances," Mosco said.

Jackal snorted. "No second chances. What else is the carnival here for but to give us our second chances? Who among us has not come to this traveling festival of misfortune for want of a second chance?"

Mosco rolled his eyes. "Save it for the bally, Jackal."

"I will not! You hired me because I'm the best talker in the game, and I respect your opinion on that matter, but I am here to tell you that I can no longer run the bally alone." He put his arm around Portia's shoulders. "And I would like this young lady to be my new assistant."

Mosco put his fork down. "What are you trying to pull? You hadn't even laid eyes on her until a minute ago."

"Nevertheless, I know a good talker when I hear one, and if this girl can tell you that ridiculous story about her Italian aunt with a straight face, then I say she belongs with me on the bally line."

"Oh, for Pete's sake."

Portia had no idea what was being discussed, but at the moment the only thing keeping her upright was Jackal's arm around her shoulder. It was dusty (all the way down to the fingertips), and it was strange, but it was also real, and she didn't have much more to count on. She certainly couldn't afford to faint a second time.

"Please, sir," she said. "I won't let you down again."

"Fine," Mosco said. "Fine. But you two split the talker's take of the box office. I am not paying her an extra share. We're barely making the nut as it is."

Jackal patted Portia's arm with his dirty hand. "We'll work it out," he said. "Good man. Enjoy your dinner."

He led Portia away before Mosco could change his mind.

As they walked, Portia said, "I do have an Italian aunt, you know."

Jackal shook his head. "Doesn't matter, my dear. What matters is what we *say* we have, and how well we say it. Remember that when you're on the line."

"The what?"

"The stage, my dear!" He dropped his arm from her shoulders and clapped his hands. "You are now in the noble business of the ballyhoo." Then he reached for her hand, shook it, and announced, "We start in the morning."

Portia spent the rest of the evening dishing out bowls of food and washing the empty bowls that returned on Violet's tray—the air in the kitchen trailer was stifling, but she was glad to be alone. Occasionally she allowed herself a look at the tables through the propped-open door, where she could view the "strange people" she would soon be selling tickets for. The shock of seeing them earlier had dulled to a tense curiosity. She knew she should not be peeking at them this way, and yet she could think of no other way to get used to them.

And if she was going to stay, she must get used to them.

Violet was clearly more comfortable, sweeping between tables and chatting with everyone as though she were running a five-star restaurant. One little boy, pale as milk, kept reaching out for her as she passed. A man and a woman with the same white translucence sat on either side of him. A family. It had been so long since Portia had seen one that she nearly forgot where she was.

Immediately after dinner service was over, Portia followed Violet back to her — their — trailer, where the red bicycle was waiting like a stray dog. Portia grazed the seat with one finger as she passed, a reluctant greeting, and went inside. The trailer was hot, but she had survived her first day and would not complain of any discomfort.

It was not so different, she told herself, than Mister's house. She cooked for people who did not thank her, she cleaned up alone, and she slept in a strange bed.

And now she found herself sharing a trailer with Violet, making up a tiny cot that dropped down from the wall and would have been barely wide enough for The Human Skeleton, featured on the bally line above the midway stage.

Another stopping point on the way back to her real life, she told herself. She would make herself remember before she fell asleep tonight, every night. Her ritual, to keep from forgetting.

"So," Violet said as she brushed out her hair, "now you know."

"Know what?"

"What we are. What we do. You sure you want to stay?"

Portia felt she was being tested. No one had asked her anything — where she had come from, why she had left, whether there was anyone looking for her — but there were questions hovering in the air like insects. "For now," she said. "Everyone seems . . . nice."

Violet murmured noncommittally.

"Who was that family?" Portia asked. "With the little boy. Are they part of the show?"

"Yes." Violet stopped brushing and turned away.

"What do they do?"

"Same thing everybody does. They sit onstage so people can stare at them."

"He . . . The boy was trying to get your attention. He seemed to care about you."

"Well, he should." Violet slid into bed and opened a magazine, obscuring her face. "He's my brother."

Exhausted as she was, Portia put off going to sleep. She dreaded the falling quiet of those first moments in bed, when she knew her mind would grow louder with its doubts and objections to what she had done. So she crept out of the trailer and stood on the steps, wondering what to do next, when Gideon appeared out of the darkness.

"Seems like dinner went okay," he offered. "I hear you're along for the ride tomorrow."

She was relieved to have been saved from her own presence. She hoped she didn't smell too strongly of the pie car. "I'm Jackal's new assistant. Whatever that means."

Gideon smiled. "Couldn't tell you. Jackal's never had an assistant before."

"Oh." Portia wrapped her — Caroline's — yellow sweater

around herself and sat on the top step of the trailer. "How long have you known him? I mean, how long have you been with the . . . show?" She wanted to add, *And what in God's name are you doing here?* But she wouldn't have known how to answer that herself. And given what Violet had just revealed, she wasn't sure she wanted to know.

Gideon sat on the ground a few feet away, just far enough into the shadows that she had to concentrate to see his face. "Since my father died," he said. "Four years ago. He lost all of his money in the crash in 'thirty-three. Never really got over it. There was no family business anymore, so I figured there was no good reason to stay." He paused. "Can I offer you some advice?"

"Sure," Portia replied.

"It's not a good idea to ask too many questions around here. People don't like to talk about themselves. They keep things close."

"Things?"

"You know. History, secrets, where they were before. What they had to do."

"You don't seem to mind."

He stood up then, brushed the seat of his pants. "I'm not one of them. It's different for me."

Portia looked around to make sure no one else was listening. "Seems like they're the ones who are different."

Gideon rubbed the back of his neck with one hand. "Good luck tomorrow," he said. And the darkness pulled over him like curtains.

GIDEON

This is subsistence living. Everyone here has just enough money to get them through the days until they get paid again. I find it strangely comforting, not to have to think too far ahead. I know what it is to have enormous wealth and lose it all at once. It doesn't matter how much you have in the bank one day, if it's gone the next.

A system of invisible money. That's what my father told me about the stock market.

"It's all in the numbers," he said. "What we manufacture is worth only as much as the system says it is. And it's not our place to toy with the system."

My father died in an institution, surrounded by other wasted men who had been betrayed by one thing or another and could not survive the loss.

Anything can be taken away from you. This is what I know to be true. So I keep only the necessities. A few books, two sets of clothes, six handkerchiefs, a shaving mirror, a straight razor, a pocketknife, a box of pencils, a bar of soap, a toothbrush, a blanket. A duffel bag to hold it all. A bit of money in my pocket.

I will not have anything more, in case some other invisible system decides to break apart and take it all away again. An occasional luxury might appear—chocolate, music, a good cigar—but you can't trust those things. Everyone here knows that. No good getting used to the easy life.

Life wasn't meant to be easy.

JACKAL

I'd suppose you're thinking a fellow like me wants nothing good from a young lady like Portia. Thinking I'm liable to take advantage. Thinking I'm working an angle of some kind. A rascal like me must always be working an angle.

But come now, I'm no con artist. I'm a storyteller. That's what talking is, standing on that little stage and calling out to people, telling them the beginning of a story and letting them finish out the rest for themselves. And as soon as Portia told me her tale, I knew she could size up an audience. Good talker's got to have that gift, and there's no school on earth where it's taught.

Of course, it won't hurt Portia's bally when we dress her up, shine her like a new penny. She'll look like Rita Hayworth's younger sister, or I've lost my touch. What I wouldn't give for anybody to look at me and think I was that innocent. Never in my whole life, friend. Never once.

Portia reminds me of my cousin Francine. She was a good girl. Never took on airs. That Violet Lucasie could have learned a manner or two from her. She died quite young, Francine, which was a special shame because she could sing like a glorified angel, she could, and everybody knew for sure she'd go and get famous someday. Poor Francine. She was down doing wash at the river with my Aunt Mabel and some of the clothes got away, and Francine, she just jumped right in and swam after them. Poor thing never saw that riverboat coming. All happened so fast. Took days to find her body, too, and that did not help Aunt Mabel, who has never been the same despite all of our best efforts.

You don't think I'm just telling tales now, do you?

I'd be sorely wounded if you did.

The Woeful Tale of Lord Mountebank

Jackal and Portia stood in front of the sideshow tent. They stood next to each other, not speaking. Portia was accustomed to silence — Aunt Sophia had been dedicated to the "speak when spoken to" philosophy, and Mister's house did not exactly inspire conversation. So Portia was not bothered that they had been standing there for several minutes without a word between them. There was plenty to keep her eyes busy in the meantime.

The stages and the podium and the faded paintings of the acts in the pit show: The Armless Girl and The Strongman and The Sword-Swallower. The banners hung high, advertising the freaks: The Irish Giant, The World's Smallest Man, The Fat Lady, The Bearded Lady, The Wild Albinos of Bora Bora. The flaps of canvas that led into the sideshow tent, waving in the breeze, beckoning to her but still keeping her out. Drawing her and repelling her with equal force.

"This is what they come to see," Jackal finally said.

"Who?" It wasn't exactly the right question. What she wanted to know was, what kind of people paid for this? To get in the tent and stare misfortune in the face?

But Jackal seemed to understand. "Nearly everyone," he said. "There are those who walk by, who've come for the circus and the menagerie and don't want to lower themselves by associating with our operation. But if fifty people pass me on the bally, I'll sell forty tickets on a bad day. Curiosity is human nature."

He pointed at the banner line. "Have you met our performers yet?"

"Some of them," Portia said.

"And?"

She tried to think of something nice to say. "They don't seem so strange once you've heard them talking to each other."

"That is precisely why they don't speak in the tent. We don't want to ruin the effect. We don't want to invite a lot of questions, either. It wasn't easy for Mrs. Collington to break the habit, but she learned, in time."

The Armless Girl painting was behind the middle stage, the largest of the three, with The Strongman on the right and The Sword-Swallower on the left. Marie was obviously the main attraction on the outside stages. Her portrait was bigger than life-size and faced the midway, as if she might leap into the audience. She looked dangerous, almost predatory. The painting of Mosco had been done on a slightly smaller scale, so he appeared more compact than he actually was. As for The Sword-Swallower . . .

"Who's that?"

"That is Charleston Granger, or so he called himself. Only he and God know his true identity, and God might be the only one who remembers, given Charleston's affinity for drink. He has left us, sorry to say."

"Did he die?" It looked obvious to Portia that it would be impossible to survive having six swords thrust down one's throat.

"No. He was recruited last year. I simply can't bring myself to take his picture down."

"Recruited?"

"By another show. A ragtag, slipshod affair. I don't know what he was thinking, going to work for those ne'er-do-wells." He shook his head. "But I digress. I was going to tell you my own story."

"I'm all ears." Portia shifted her weight and tried to ignore the grass tickling her ankles.

"Long have I traveled these roads," Jackal said with a heavy sigh, "and long have I waited for the day when I could lay my burden down."

"Just tell me the story," Portia said irritably. "It's too hot for all the dramatic parts."

Jackal whipped his cane against the tent. The snap of the wood on the canvas was like a gunshot. "The dramatic *parts*," he said, "are the entire point of the exercise. Now sit down and listen, or I'll send you back to the pie car."

Fine with me, she thought, but it really wasn't, so she did as she was told.

"Now, where was I? Ah, yes. I was born at the dawn of the century, the fifth son of Lord and Lady Mountebank, a displaced nobleman and his ailing wife. My mother, rest her soul, barely survived my entrance into the world. My father worked as a traveling salesman to support us, and my mother was very lonely, but we were poor and my father had no choice. Each time he left, more and more time passed before he returned.

My mother and my four brothers and I waited patiently in our one-room shanty in the middle of the prairie—"

"How can you remember all this if you were just a baby?"

"Don't interrupt," he snapped. "There we waited, half starved, all alone. My father was days overdue, and it seemed neither hope nor salvation would ever find us, when there came a knock at the door. A man and his wife, making the journey from Vermont to California, had stopped to ask for shelter for the night. My mother was weak, but she was also very kind, and so she invited them in.

"The woman told my mother how much she wanted a family, how she had lost hope of having any children of her own. 'We will have a big house in California,' she said, 'with many empty rooms. It nearly breaks my heart.' She looked at my brothers and me. 'You are very lucky,' the woman told my mother, 'to have so many strong sons.'

"'I fear they will not be strong much longer,' my mother told her. 'For we are very poor, as you can see, and I am not long for this world. My husband has been gone for many days, and I think he may not come back.'"

"Is this supposed to be a true story?" Portia inquired. "Because, frankly, it's more than a little unbelievable."

Jackal glared at her.

"Sorry," she said. "Keep going."

"When the man and the woman departed in the morning, they took my brothers and me with them. They tried to take my mother, too, but she was too weak to leave the shanty. 'I will wait here for my husband,' she said. 'Whether he finds me dead or alive, I cannot say.' And so my brothers and I were carried west to begin our new life."

"Did your father ever get back to the shanty?"

"He did," said Jackal. "He found my mother alone, and when she told him what she had done, he was so overcome with rage and grief that he shot her. And then he turned the gun on himself."

"What? I thought he was so kind and —"

"No, no, it was my *mother* who was kind. My father was not a nice man. And word has it he was a terrible salesman."

"How much of that story is true?" Portia asked.

Jackal waved the question away as if it were a mosquito. "What does that matter? Truth is not what the audience wants. They want tragedy, adventure, misfortune for the rich and glory for the poor. And" — he winked — "a little murder doesn't hurt."

"So," said Portia, "if your father was Lord Mountebank and he's dead, does that mean you're Lord Mountebank now?"

"Why, it surely does, my dear."

Portia stood up and brushed the dry grass off her skirt. "And who does that make me?" she asked.

"Whoever you want to be," Jackal said, and he tipped his hat and was gone.

WHY SHE WAS THERE

Though she was sure Jackal's story was utterly untrue, it had been so long since anyone had told her a story that she turned his over and over in her mind. Worried it like a stone in her pocket. Smoothed the edges, felt all around it, until it became like a fairy tale she'd heard as a child. The story sparked inside her, igniting others, the ones she had spoken to Max and the ones she had never spoken to anyone, until it seemed that she might actually split open from so many words.

She found Gideon on the border of the midway, sitting on a water barrel and gazing toward the big top. "Better not let Mosco find you like that," she said lightly. She knew, already, that there was always something to be done, some chore, some form of motion needed to keep the circus on schedule. Sitting still was rarely an option.

Gideon smiled. "I can always tell him I'm on clown patrol."

Portia smiled, too. She didn't know what to say next. She felt—not nervous exactly, but restless, jittery.

"You finished with Jackal already?" Gideon asked.

"I guess so. For today. I'm not sure what I'm supposed to be learning from him. All he told me was a story about—"

"Lord Mountebank?"

"Yes. I thought you said people here didn't like to talk about themselves."

"Well, for one thing, Jackal's not quite like everybody else. And for another, that story's not really about Jackal. That story's been bumping around since the talker before the talker *before* Jackal. According to Doula."

"I figured," Portia said. "Still, it was interesting."

Gideon wiped at his forehead with the back of one hand, then shaded his eyes and looked toward the circus again. "First o'Mays think everything's interesting around here. Especially the sideshow."

"First of what?"

"First o'May. Somebody who signs on with the circus because they're curious. Or in trouble. Running away from something, usually."

"Is that what you think I am?"

"Aren't you? Nothing wrong with it."

But it sounded wrong to Portia, like an insult or a bad joke, to be so easily identified with other strangers. People who had come and gone and left no mark. People who had simply disappeared into the past and never been seen again.

"You don't know anything about me," she snapped. "You don't know why I'm here or where I've come from, and you don't want to know. You want me to keep my secrets? Fine. But don't accuse me of hiding something when you're the one who told me to mind my own business."

"I didn't—" Gideon started, but Portia was already striding away.

"Wait!" he shouted, and then she heard his feet thumping

the dry ground as he ran up behind her and grabbed her shoulder. His hold was firm, but careful, and Portia willed herself to stand still, to feel her own bones beneath his hand, before turning to face him.

"I didn't mean—" he stammered. "I'm sorry. It's just that I've seen a lot of folks come through here, acting like they care about the show and then running off again. Couple of 'em turned out to be reporters. Just wanted to take pictures of the freaks and put them in the newspaper." He scuffed his shoe in the dirt. "There aren't that many good reasons for normals wanting to join up with the sideshow, y'know. Mostly they're after something."

He looked at her.

"That's not why I'm here," Portia said quietly.

"Then why?"

"I—" The words, again, pushed at her from the inside, wanting to get out. "I'm looking for my father."

Gideon seemed relieved, as if he'd been afraid that Portia's reason was something insidious, something much worse than a lost parent. "Does he work for the circus?"

It was a simple question, one that Portia had tried not to ask herself too directly. Because the truth was that she did not know whether Max really had joined up with a circus, much less *this* circus. She did not know if he was here, or within a thousand miles of here, or even if he was alive. Her throat burned, and she swallowed hard.

"I don't know where he is," she whispered. "I just . . . I had to find a place to look for him. And he loved the circus, once."

"It's as good a place as any," Gideon said, "to look for someone. You'll see, tonight. It's empty now, but pretty soon there'll be people everywhere, more than you can count. I can help you, if you want."

She shook her head, but smiled. "Jackal wants me by the stage, so I can keep an eye out."

"Well, I'm working the ticket wagon tonight, so I'll see everyone except the folks who sneak in. If you change your mind—"

"Thank you," Portia said. She couldn't say why, but she felt that this was her work to do, that if anyone was going to find Max in the crowd, it should be her. It must be her. Besides, how could she describe him to Gideon, tell him who to look for, when she didn't have a picture to show? Even the picture in her head was more than five years old, and five years could change a person. She doubted Max would recognize *her*.

She could only hope that, if he did set foot on the midway that night, she would find a way to see him, to know him, and this time, not to let him leave without her.

INSIDE

That evening Portia went inside for the first time.

Jackal said she needed to observe his methods before she could make any attempt at her own bally, and he told her to bring a quarter for admission. But Portia was not about to surrender any of her precious savings to follow Jackal's orders, even with the added bonus of finally having her curiosity satisfied. It was unheard of for Jackal to give anybody anything for free. But he had become addicted to having a pupil. So he relented, and Portia became the only nonpaying sideshow spectator in the history of the Wonder Show.

The crowd had been drawn, as they were meant to be, by Mosco's and Marie's acts. They were the pit show, designed to entice passing rubes with their strange and marvelous tricks. Portia stood to one side of the stage. She thought again of The Pinhead and the accordion, the strains of tinny music reaching her ears as she sat high on the stranger's shoulders. She glanced at the faces below—she could see everyone, but it was like looking into a forest from far away, impossible to distinguish one tree from another. Still, she scanned the crowd, searching for anyone she recognized.

It would be impossible to find someone, Portia thought, *if you lost them here.* She looked again behind the carnival games, past the place where she knew the trucks were parked, into the blackest dark. And she felt such despair that she had to close her eyes.

The night voices threatened to speak again, and she fought them off.

One night at a time, she told herself. *The world is smaller than it seems.*

As Anna gathered her sister Marie's knives and exited the stage, the rubes whispered and shuffled nervously, unsure of what they would see next.

And Jackal went to work.

"Ladies and gentlemen, boys and girls, friends and neighbors," he bellowed, "allow me to change your lives!"

It was key to have an opening line that was just this side of unbelievable. Did the rubes think their lives would really change because of what was in the tent? Of course not. Did they want to risk missing out, just in case it was something truly spectacular? Of course not.

Portia saw the midway crowd draw almost imperceptibly closer. Elevated above them, in his blinding white suit and bowler, both hands on the podium as if he were just barely able to contain his excitement, Jackal looked every bit like the preacher salesman that he was.

"That's right, folks, change your lives, that's what I said. For inside the tent behind me sits a stage full of the strangest people you have ever seen. Seeing is believing, folks, but you won't believe your eyes. It's the most marvelous collection of human oddities this side of the equator."

A murmur rippled across the crowd, equal parts doubt and interest. This was the balance Jackal wanted to upset in his favor. "It's like making cheese," he'd told Portia. "You want to skim the bad stuff off the top and get to the parts that'll give you what you want." The first to go: anyone with young children.

"Not for the faint of heart, folks," Jackal warned. "If you're prone to nightmares or you've got a weak ticker, you'd best move on."

A few mothers clucked their tongues and gathered their offspring immediately. "Let's go see the elephants again," one said.

"I wanna see the freaks!" her son wailed.

The woman gave Jackal a disapproving look over her shoulder as she led the disappointed boy away by the arm. Portia smiled a little, thinking of the mothers of Brewster Falls calling their children away from the road when she came flying by on the red bicycle.

"That's okay, son," Jackal called after them. "You come back by yourself next year!"

Some of the men in the crowd chuckled.

"Listen up, folks. We've got a six-in-one to beat the band. This is what your neighbors will be talking about at the grocery store and the dancehall, and even" — Jackal winked — "at the church social. This is what you'll tell your grandkids about when they ask you for your best stories. They'll say, 'Tell me a story,' and you'll say, 'Have I told you about the time I saw the fattest woman in the world and The Wild Albinos of Bora Bora?' Yes, sir. Yes, ma'am. This is where it's at."

He lowered his voice just a bit, hitting a conspiratorial tone.

"And would you believe you can see every one of these marvel-ous marvels for only a quarter?"

The next to go: anyone without a quarter. Or the willing-ness to spend it.

There was still a decently large crowd, though, and Jackal gestured to the podium, where Anna waited to collect the money in a tin can while he went inside to wait for his audience.

Portia stepped off the side of the stage and joined the slow herd of spectators entering the six-in-one.

It was hot.

It smelled like sawdust.

The crowd inched forward as if they had been set to slow motion.

It was darker than the waning day outside, and the sounds dimmed, too. None of the happy chatter, the vendors calling out, the music, the animals. There was only the low buzz of urgent whispers, the occasional stifled laugh. And then, before Portia's eyes had even adjusted, Jackal began to speak. "Step in, step in, folks! Plenty of room for everyone!"

Portia could see now that the tent was much bigger than it needed to be. It was mostly empty, even with Jackal's voice pouring into every corner. There was one long stage laid down the middle, like a giant dining room table, with room on all sides for walking around. Room for the rubes to see the freaks from every angle. The entrance brought them to the front of the stage, where Mrs. Murphy sat in a plush blue wingback chair.

Portia knew she should be listening to Jackal—that was why he had let her in, so she could witness his ballyhoo—but something about seeing her new companions at work, lined up on the stage like a buffet, made it difficult to concentrate.

Mrs. Murphy was looking very intently into her lap, and as Portia was drawn forward, she saw the woman's hands moving steadily, rhythmically. Needlepoint. She was working on her needlepoint.

Portia thought of the dozens of needlepoint pillows in Mrs. Murphy's trailer and began to feel a little ill.

There was a small placard fixed to the front of the stage. EMMELINE MURPHY, it said. BEARDED LADY.

The man in front of her elbowed his friend. "Her beard's better-looking than yours, Fred!" They both barked with laughter.

He's right, Portia thought. Mrs. Murphy's beard was red and gold, so silky it glowed like an oil painting.

Still, Mrs. Murphy did not look up.

Mrs. Collington, on the other hand, smiled and waved so the flesh under her arm danced hypnotically. No one waved back, so Portia raised her hand to say hello, but the expression on Mrs. Collington's face didn't change, even a little bit. Then Portia realized that she wasn't waving to the crowd. Or at least, she wasn't looking at the crowd. She was looking over their heads — giving the appearance of being happy to see them, of being the friendly, jolly fat lady they expected and had paid to see.

MRS. COLLINGTON, her placard said. 800 POUNDS.

Jimmy and Jim were, of course, next to each other, labeled WORLD'S SMALLEST MAN and IRISH GIANT. Portia wondered if Jim was in fact the tallest man in the world but had to admit she'd never seen anyone taller and probably neither had anyone else in the crowd, so who were they to argue? He looked rather sad and resigned to sitting there and letting people stare at his ankles, which showed because his pants were never long enough. Even though he made them himself. He always under-estimated how tall he really was.

Jimmy could have had the opposite problem, out of wishing to be taller, but his clothes fit him flawlessly. He was very dis-tinguished from toe to neck and all scowls above the collar. He gave Portia an especially fierce glare, and she glared back until the crowd forced her to keep walking.

Move along, the crowd was saying. *Let us be done with this. And get a good long look while we're here.*

So on they went, past the WILD ALBINOS OF BORA BORA, who stood like dignified statues. Even Joseph. On they went, whispering, pointing, laughing nervously, until they came to the end of the stage and found themselves at a dark curtain. Jackal was waiting.

"Behind this door," he said, low so everyone had to strain to hear him, "is the sixth and greatest act in our distinguished display. A true wonder of nature awaits you. The sight is yours for a single dollar. One dollar, folks. That's all it'll cost you for a once-in-a-lifetime experience. But I warn you: you will never be the same after this. Enter. If. You. Dare.

"Otherwise," he added in a flat tone, "you may exit to my right."

About half of the crowd had had enough wonders of nature already. No one complained about having paid a quarter and seeing only five freaks. They simply extracted themselves and walked silently, carefully out of the tent, back to the evening light and the midway and the normal things of the normal world they lived in. There was a burst of noise when the tent flap was lifted, and then it dropped and the close quiet of this other realm was restored.

"Now," Jackal said, grinning, "we see who the real men are."

For it was only men who remained. Except for Portia.

Perhaps they had heard the stories of other carnivals, had heard about the blowoff, the final act in the freak show that cost extra and often involved some half-naked exotic woman. A woman with a tail or a third breast. A woman who was somehow both a woman and a man, top half and bottom half or, even stranger, divided down the middle.

Portia knew better, though. Because she hadn't seen Polly and Pippa on the stage with the rest of the cast. And they had to be somewhere.

Portia waited until all the men were through and stepped up to Jackal. He gave her the eyebrow again.

"End of the line for you," he said.

"Jackal," she said. "Let me through."

"Not a bloody chance," he replied. There was something behind his smile, a secret behind a steel door. He would not relent, Portia could see that. But she had rarely come to a door and not tried to open it.

"But you want me to know," she reminded him. "You want me to bring the customers back here. I have to know what I'm talking about, don't I?"

"Go," he told her. "Walk around. Blend in. Listen up. See what they're seeing, how they're seeing it. You've got to know your audience."

"I've seen the lot. I know it already."

"Not at night, you don't. You haven't seen anything until you've seen the lot at night." Jackal pointed at the exit and smiled again. "It's that way."

Then, as she turned to go, he spat, "And they're not *customers*. They're *rubes*. Don't ever forget that."

Brotherly Love

Joseph Lucasie was a strange boy. Even though his skin and hair were utterly white, aside from his dark glasses and his sun umbrella, he was strange. In the five days since her arrival, Portia had never seen him speak to anyone except Violet, not even his parents, and she frequently caught him glaring at her for no apparent reason.

"I don't think your brother likes me," Portia told Violet. They were wearing lost-and-found sunglasses, sitting in lost-and-found lawn chairs in front of their trailer, trying to keep from falling through the worn-out fabric. The heat was like a blanket. Violet fanned herself with a movie magazine.

"He doesn't like anyone," Violet said. "Only me. Lucky, lucky me."

"Doesn't he have any friends?"

"There aren't any kids around except the ones who come for the circus, and they're not going to make friends with someone like Joseph. They might talk to me, but he always shows up and scares them off. It might not be so bad if he made an effort, but he just stands there and stares and doesn't say anything. It spooks people. I've tried to tell him. People are going to think he's touched in the head or something."

Portia blushed. That was exactly what she'd thought.

"Anyway," Violet said, "he'll have to learn to fend for himself sometime. I'm not here to spend my life being his only friend. I've got better things to do."

"Like what?" Maybe she could give Portia a few ideas.

"Anything. Everything. I want to be an actress. I want to learn to fly a plane. I want to take a train from one coast to the other and see the whole country."

"I'll bet you've seen a lot more of the country than I have," Portia said.

"We mostly go in circles around the middle," Violet said. "I want to see it all at once. And not from a broken-down truck hauling a broken-down trailer. I want to see it whiz past me like a shooting star. Then I'll know I'm really moving. And I want to see it on my own."

"Why do you have to stay in the middle?"

Violet adjusted her sunglasses. "The big shows have the rest of it staked out, and we're not allowed to get too deep into their territory. They've got better acts than we do, too. Elephants and big cats, plus the best freaks in the business. It's really not fair." She sighed deeply. "It was better when the Wonder Show was a ten-in-one."

"A what?"

"A sideshow with ten acts. Ten freaks inside the tent, that's a ten-in-one. Then Edwina the Lobster Girl ran off with Rafael the Rubber-Skinned Man, and The Human Torso went with another show, and The Human Skeleton died."

"How'd he die?"

"Food poisoning. Bad meat or something." Violet sounded almost on the verge of laughter. "Anyway, now Mosco's only got a six-in-one. He's still got some good acts, but competition's stiff, and The Human Torso was really something special. He rolled cigarettes with just his lips, and he did it faster than most men do with their hands. Good and tight, too. Mosco sold 'em as souvenirs."

Portia shifted carefully in her chair. "Wouldn't you miss your family? If you left?"

"I don't know," Violet said vacantly. "I've never had a chance to be away from them."

Portia tried to imagine it for her then, pictured Violet riding in a train all alone, flying past the towns she'd been through with the caravan. Maybe she'd see the carnival on the road somewhere along the tracks. Maybe Joseph would look out the truck window at the same time Violet looked out the train, and they would see each other for an instant. Portia wasn't sure she liked Joseph, but it was rather sad to think of him having to watch his only friend hurtling away from him on a speeding train.

As if she'd summoned him with her mind, Joseph came around the trailer and called for Violet. It was the first time Portia had heard his voice—it was surprisingly high and sweet. It didn't match his scowl when he saw Portia sitting there.

"What are you talking about?" Joseph demanded.

"None of your business," Violet replied. "It's girl talk."

"You're supposed to be helping me with my multiplication tables."

"Fine. What's five times six?"

Joseph crossed his arms. "Not in front of her."

Violet rolled her eyes, but Portia said, "That's all right. I told Jackal I would help him paint the stage." She stood up and said, "Here, Joseph, you can have my seat."

"What do you say, Joseph?" Violet prodded.

"You know I can't sit out here," he snapped.

It took all of Portia's self-control not to snap back. *He's just a kid*, she told herself. "I didn't know," she said.

"He can't be in the sun." Violet swatted Joseph with her magazine. "This is what I have to deal with. I'm telling you, the minute I get the chance, I am gone."

The change in Joseph was instantaneous. He dropped to his knees and his umbrella tipped, exposing one ear to the sun. "I'm sorry!" he said. "I'm sorry I was rude, Violet, I'm sorry!" He looked as though he might actually cry, even though Portia was still standing there. She knew something about not letting yourself cry in front of certain people, what it took to keep your chin steady and your eyes clear.

"God, Joseph," Violet said, "you're so dramatic. Just forget it, okay? I'm not going anywhere. Now, what's five times six?"

Portia could hear their voices carrying on the wind as she walked away, Violet's gruff and Joseph's sweet, like instruments harmonizing. They were family, parts of the same orchestra. But when she looked back at them over her shoulder, she saw how different they were, too. Violet's black hair and dark skin made Joseph look even more like a ghost. Portia looked down at her own arms, brown from working in the sun, and she saw them as if they belonged to someone else. They were regular arms. Strong, young, normal arms, the kind that Marie might have had in another life.

But here, in this place, normal meant nothing. No one paid money to see normal, no one made a living from it. Portia had seen the freaks making a fuss over Joseph, the only young one among them, telling him how special he was while Violet stood by the pie car, the sun shining on her golden skin.

Violet could have things that Joseph and their parents could not have. The world outside would welcome her, but only if she left her family behind. And from what Portia could tell, Violet was perfectly willing to pay that price.

She wondered what Max had been thinking the day he drove away on the road of dust. Was he watching the land fly past and the horizon at the end of the sky, coming to meet him? Was he glancing in that rearview mirror every now and then, or was he looking straight ahead and thinking about a whole new life?

It shouldn't be so easy to leave a place, Portia thought. But then she realized that if it weren't so easy, she'd still be at Mister's. Caroline tapped at the edge of her memory, and Sophia, and Quintillia, and all the others. The ones who left, and the ones who were left behind, everyone in motion like startled birds, trying to find a place to land.

GIRL ON THE INSIDE

"Ladies and gentlemen, friends and neighbors," Portia called.

"Louder! Drop your voice!"

She made her voice deep and bellowed, "Ladies and gentle-men—"

"Louder!"

"LADIES—"

Jackal trotted back from where he'd been standing. "It seems I've made a cardinal error."

"What are you talking about?"

"I neglected to check your qualifications before I gave you the job."

"But I know all the lines. I've learned everything you told me to say."

Jackal nodded. "That is true, and for that, I commend you. However, no one gives a whit what you're saying if they. Can't. Hear. You."

Portia imagined waking up one morning and finding herself alone on the lot, abandoned by the Wonder Show. "I can do it. Go back over there and let me try again." She pushed at

Jackal's shoulder, but he stood solid as a closed door and gazed thoughtfully into the air.

"No," he said. "It won't work. Your voice simply isn't strong enough."

Portia crossed her arms and pinched the insides of her elbows to keep herself from crying. Or shouting. She felt she might do either at any moment. "Jackal, please."

He tilted his head and smiled wickedly. "Why, darling, I do believe your heart has leaped onto your sleeve. Have you grown so attached to me already?"

"Forget it," she said, and turned to walk away.

"Now, now," Jackal said. "I'm only teasing."

"It's not funny," she mumbled. But she turned back, and Jackal bowed in exaggerated apology.

"I am *deeply* sorry," he said.

"I can see that. Get up. Come on."

He hopped back to standing and said, "Apology is good for the soul. I try to apologize at least once a day."

"Have you ever tried not doing anything you'd have to apologize for?"

"Absolutely not. Now, about your little vocal problem . . ."

"What about a microphone?"

Jackal shook his head vehemently. "No, no, and no. It distorts the voice, and it is a scientific fact that speaking through an audio device makes you fifty percent less trustworthy in the eyes of your fellow man. You must speak directly to the ears of your audience, nothing between you."

"Nothing except a bunch of stories that are barely true."

"Barely true is still true enough," he said. "Now be quiet so I can think."

Quiet was not much of a possibility on the lot. There was always a symphony of sounds, even between shows: voices everywhere, truck motors and the hum of the generators, hammers pounding tent stakes, horses, elephants, tigers grunting in the heat, circus mothers calling circus children, the bell from the pie car pinging faintly in the wind, music from dozens of radios, layering into one another, clustering like leaves on a branch. A steady combination of noises that equaled quiet, the ever-present purr in the background.

And right now it was the sound of Jackal deciding Portia's future.

She waited.

Jackal paced.

She waited some more.

"Good girl," he said finally. "I think I've got it."

"And?"

"We'll switch places," he said. "You'll be the inside talker and I'll do the bally. It's perfect, actually—I don't know why I didn't think of it before. I bring them in, you lead them through, and I meet you at the other end for the blowoff."

"But what do I have to do?"

"The rubes will adore having a girl in there with them, a soft voice, making them comfortable." Jackal was hopping around like a boy on Christmas morning. "Oh, the contrast! Between you and the ones on stage! We'll have Mrs. Collington make you a new dress. A white one. Oh, I'm breathless with the perfection of it! I think I need to sit down."

"Jackal, what will I say?"

"Just what I taught you. Same sad stories, only now you'll be standing right in front of the freaks."

"I wish you wouldn't call them that."

Jackal smirked. "What should I call them? The talent? The artists?"

"They're people."

"Darling, we're all people. That is not the point. There are three parts of the Wonder Show: the human marvels, the freaks, and the talkers. We all know who we are in the show, and who we are when the show is over." He jabbed a finger at the bally line. "This is the show, and this show has freaks. You see?"

"Yes, I see."

Jackal shook his head. "No, you don't. Not yet. But you will." He leaned in and tapped the tip of her nose. "Once you're inside."

Resisting the urge to slap his hand away, Portia smiled sweetly and did not move. In her time with Jackal — indeed, in her time with the entire show — she had learned that it was better to conceal her thoughts until the right moment. She was a guest here, a temporary passenger, and she could not leave too large a mark. Mister had surely sent someone to fetch her by now. She could not risk offending those who were willing to help her hide.

Even if they didn't know, or want to know, whom she was hiding from.

Just a little more time, she thought as she made her way to the pie car. *I'll find Max, I know it. I just need a little more time.*

FORTUNETELLING

In Portia's dream, she had sisters, and their parents were missionaries who took them to live in a warm place. There was a monastery nearby. It was a country made of hills.

There was a family who had sons, and it was decided somehow that the boy called Everett was intended for Portia's older sister. But when he came, he didn't want her. He wanted Portia.

She knew she would have to leave her family in order to make things right. It was the first dream Portia could remember in such a long time that she asked Doula about it.

Doula shrugged her left shoulder, which meant she had an idea but didn't want to say. A right-shoulder shrug meant she really had nothing to tell. Portia knew the code only because Jackal got mad at Doula one day after he asked her for the winning horses and all she told him was to quit gambling. Like a child having a tantrum, he told Portia the only one of Doula's secrets he knew. This was the first time it had proven useful.

"Doula," Portia said. "Please."

"Maybe . . ."

The world paused under her feet.

"Maybe you know is time for you to go."

"But I don't want to go," Portia said unevenly. "I just got here."

Doula tapped her glass, and Portia poured more vodka from the bottle on the table. "Why should you get to choose? The rest of us, we go where someone else tells us. We follow circus, circus follows route card, route card is made by some big man in New York City. We don't choose." She tossed her head, and her earrings sang. "You will learn if you stay here. You will see."

"Can you tell me anything else? About my dream? What it means?"

Doula emptied her glass with one practiced flip of the hand, set it back on the table, and leaned back in her chair. "You think you are the first orphan to dream about family? It means you miss them. It means you are looking."

"I'm not an orphan," Portia said. (She hoped it was true.)

Doula shrugged both shoulders. Portia didn't know what that meant.

"Do you . . ."

"What?"

"Do you think I'll find them?"

Doula shrugged. "Sometimes, is a very big world. Sometimes, very small."

It was the kind of answer that wasn't an answer. But it was all Portia would get that day.

The bottle was empty.

DOULA

I know what Portia want, sure. Want someone tell her what to do. Maybe she don't know why she come back to me day after day, asking questions. She don't ask one question, most important question, see? She ask *around* the question. Getting close, maybe. I don't push.

I learn that a long time ago, was something my grandmother told me. She said these people, they think they want to know the future. They come in, pay you money, ask, "Does he love me? Does she miss me? What will happen?" But who wants to hear the truth? No one. Is only not knowing the truth keeps life interesting. Makes life possible to go on.

So I don't tell her what I see around her.

But she got a ghost. A girl. I see this girl all around Portia everywhere she is, close to her side every day. I don't tell her. Maybe Portia know this girl is there. I think she can feel her, and this is why her dreams become strange.

The ghosts, they don't need to sleep. They wait for their people to sleep, and the door between the worlds, it opens then, and the ghosts send their messages. Their people don't always listen, but the ghosts will not give up.

They got nothing but time. They got nothing else to do but try to make themselves heard. And this girl ghost, she is not done with Portia yet.

I will tell Portia this, sure.

If she ask me.

DINING, CARNIVAL STYLE

They ate after the roustabouts and the circus performers. One group did not mix with another, and everyone had their own opinion on why that was.

"They can't stand to look at us," Jimmy said, as sourly as he said most things.

"That's not why," Anna said softly.

"Aw," Jimmy snapped, "what do you know? You're normal-looking."

"Except when she's getting knives thrown at her," Polly pointed out. "That's just plain scary."

Pippa rolled her eyes.

It was the breakfast shift. They were all sitting around the long wooden table on the long wooden benches that often put splinters in their backsides. The air in the meal tent was hot and heavy with the smell of fry oil. No matter what she and Violet tried to do, everything that came out of the pie car tasted as if it had been deep-fried. Even the scrambled eggs.

"I think," Marie said, "they don't care what we look like. They are used to looking at us by now, yes?" She directed the question at Mosco, who was sitting opposite her and apparently eating his eggs without chewing.

Swallowing hard, he said, "Yes. I mean, no. I mean, circus folks don't care what anybody looks like. Far as they're concerned, they're the only ones in the world."

"Is that true?" Portia asked Gideon quietly.

"Course it's true!" Mosco bellowed. "Don't bother whispering around me, girl, 'cause I got ears like a bat and I hear everything."

"You got eyes like a bat, too?" Portia retorted.

"What's that supposed to mean?"

Marie laughed. "She means you are blind, Mosco. She means you don't see what's right in front of you."

"I see plenty," Mosco said. "Like right now, for instance, I see the whole bunch of you sitting around a table like you're on vacation or something."

"All right," Gideon said. "We're going." He grabbed Portia's arm and pulled her away from the tent.

"Hey!" she yelped.

Gideon ignored it. "If you're smart, and you seem to think you are, you won't bait Mosco like that."

"I wasn't baiting him," Portia said. "I just don't like being treated like a child."

"Well, this is how it works around here: you've got to prove you're not a child before anyone will treat you like anything else. In case you hadn't noticed, you're the youngest one here, except for Joseph. And you can't expect to show up on your little red bicycle and have everyone think you're a grownup."

She glared at him.

"What?" he said.

"Now *you're* doing it."

"Sorry."

"Good," she said. "And none of you know a thing about where I come from, so you can just stick it in your ear."

"Real mature," he called after her, as she stalked away.

She knew he was right. That was the worst part, really. She couldn't afford to be singled out or, worse, told to leave. Did that happen here? Did everyone get to stay until they wanted out, or could they be banned from the kingdom? Where would she go?

She was so preoccupied with the noise of these questions, she did not hear Gideon coming, catching up just as she reached her trailer. The short walk through the heavy humid air had, lucky for him, taken most of the fight out of her. Now she just felt limp.

"I'm sorry," he started, but she waved it away.

"You don't have to," she told him. "You were right. I should have kept my mouth shut." She smiled ruefully. "That has never been one of my talents."

He ran one hand through his shaggy hair, then did it again. "How about a haircut? Is that one of your talents?"

"I don't know. I've never done it before."

"Be right back," Gideon said, and trotted off, returning after a few minutes with a pair of scissors, a comb, and two small mirrors. "So I can check the back," he said, holding them up and smiling. "Keep an eye on you."

"Are you sure about this?" Portia asked him. "You trust me to do this?"

"Any reason I shouldn't?"

I killed my best friend, she thought. *How about that?*

Then she shook her head and held her hand out for the scissors and the comb. "None that I can think of. Sit."

She perched on the trailer steps, and Gideon plunked down in the dirt in front of her. His hair had always just looked brown, and often dusty, but now she could see strands of gold running through it, glinting in the sun. The back of his neck was smooth, vulnerable. She was tempted to rest her fingertips there, just for a second; instead, she brushed her own hair away from her face with the back of her hand, flicked the comb into place, and began to trim.

For a few minutes, the only sound between them was the raspy voice of the scissors. Portia was cautious with her cutting, though she suspected Gideon wouldn't care if his hair was even or not. It looked as if he had performed his last haircut himself.

"So, any luck?" he said.

"I think I'm getting it," she answered. "It's kind of a mess back here."

He laughed. "Not my hair. Finding your father. Any luck so far?"

"Oh." Her scissors paused. "No. Not yet."

"Well, you've got time," he said reassuringly. "Plenty of stops left before the show heads south for the winter."

Portia wasn't so certain. She had seen other girls, other runaways, return to The Home in the custody of expressionless men in dark suits, driving dark cars. Had seen Mister giving them money and shaking their hands, thanking them for bringing back his charges. He did not take kindly to girls leaving his house without permission. And the girls who were brought back had a way of disappearing again. In her bunk-house stories, Portia had made Mister into Bluebeard, a secret killer. After what she had seen in the graveyard, she wondered if she had been closer to the truth than she'd meant to be.

But she did not say any of this to Gideon. She did not say anything.

He held one mirror over his shoulder so she could see his eyes and she knew he could see hers. "Don't give up," he said. "This can be a magical place."

"Now who sounds like a child?" she said, and pushed his hand away.

FROM THE NOTEBOOK OF PORTIA REMINI

Where We Have Been	What I Am Tired Of
Dixon	Potatoes
Freeport	Driving
Dubuque	Dust
Maquoketa	Waiting
Davenport	
Muscatine	
Macomb	

ANGRY

Jimmy hated everything. Or so it seemed. Since Portia had met him, he had expressed a biting hatred for Hollywood, televisions, telephones, sewing machines, women with red hair, men who wore cowboy hats, children, the smell of cigar smoke, steps, ladders, heat, working indoors, sleeping outdoors, cats, dogs, elephants, horses, and clowns. It was a matter of course that he hated some of these things, like the steps, which presented a struggle on a near-daily basis. The rest made Portia wonder why Jimmy stuck around the carnival.

Perhaps because there was a steady supply of the only things Jimmy didn't hate, which were cigarettes and whiskey and Jim.

The dwarf and the giant went everywhere together. Jimmy had finally conquered Jim's habit of offering to carry him around — he appreciated how much easier it would have been to get around, but he couldn't abide people staring and pointing, and after their picture appeared in *Billboard* with the caption IRISH GIANT AND SON, Jimmy told Jim he'd walk on his own feet or stay where he was.

Jim pointed out that the photograph had been an honest mistake, probably due to the fact that they were wearing matching pants. (They often ordered trousers made of the same fabric so that after Jimmy cut the legs off his, Jim could sew the extra material onto his cuffs and have pants that were nearly the proper length.) Nevertheless, Jimmy's pride had been wounded, and like the elephants he detested, he possessed an extremely long and accurate memory. It kept his pain fresh. It did not allow him to forgive.

He preferred it that way.

Portia knew how to recognize the faces of the wounded, and she knew how to steer herself around them so they did not notice her. Living in Mister's house had cultivated that skill. Being in the orbit of an unpredictable planet, one that could explode or veer off course at any moment, had taught her to feel for the energy in a room before she entered it. If the room felt hot, she would step carefully as if walking through a minefield. If the room crackled and hissed, she would not go in at all.

The carnival was just like any other house, really. The trailers were the bedrooms, the pie car was the kitchen, the outside spaces in between were the hallways and the alcoves. The bally was the front porch, and the sideshow tent was the parlor where guests were received. Portia could feel the energy of each part of this house, just the way she had navigated her way through Mister's. And she felt the energy of the inhabitants as well.

So she sidestepped Jimmy, until he cornered her and demanded to know what her problem was.

Portia was genuinely flummoxed. "I beg your pardon?"

"Ah," Jimmy spat, "you never begged for anything in your life." And apparently he considered their conversation finished, because he walked off in the direction of his truck.

Portia, however, had spent several days intermittently working with Jackal and peeling potatoes until her fingers pruned, and she was in no mood for Jimmy's hit-and-run abuse.

"Get back here!" she hollered.

He didn't even slow down. So she strode after him, but somehow, despite his lack of stature, she couldn't manage to catch up with him. It was as if she were in one of those dreams where she'd forgotten how to walk and every step was a concerted mental effort. Jimmy didn't stop until he got to his and Jim's truck.

They'd pooled their money to buy it, and modified it themselves so they didn't have to rely on anyone else to drive. The truck, like Jimmy, seemed designed to repel anyone curious enough to come near it. It was spotted with rust, and the windows were thoroughly scratched, as if the previous owner had regularly massaged the truck with sandpaper and handfuls of gravel. Jim and Jimmy liked it that way. They knew it wouldn't get stolen, and the truck being in the condition it was, they hadn't felt any guilt about cutting the front seat in half.

The passenger side of the front seat had been discarded. Jim could sit in the back and stretch his legs clear through. He could easily have reached the pedals, if the absent half of the seat had been on the driver's side, but Jimmy was convinced Jim didn't have the attention span to drive (even though Jim had patiently tailored every one of Jimmy's suits). So he strapped wood blocks to the gas, the brake, and the clutch and brought the remaining half of the front seat as close to the steering wheel as it would go. He got himself a thick soft cushion so he could see over the dashboard, and it was this cushion he settled into now as he blatantly ignored Portia's attempts to get his attention.

Finally her fist against the glass was too much for him. He

rolled down the window—a process that seemed to take the better part of an hour.

"What?!"

"Don't you yell at me," Portia hollered. "You started this."

"And I'm finishing it." He sneered and started to roll the window back up. Portia stuck her hand through the gradually shrinking gap.

"You think I won't crush your hand like a walnut?" Jimmy inquired. "Because I will. I'll do it."

She left her hand where it was, hovering between glass and frame.

It was a proper standoff.

And Portia was victorious.

"Bah," he muttered, and slapped both hands against the steering wheel. "Ain't even worth the effort."

She tried not to smile when she asked, "You done now?"

He didn't answer, just leaned over the empty space where the passenger seat used to be, opened the glove compartment, and extracted a crushed pack of cigarettes. He pushed the lighter button on the dashboard and thrust the pack at Portia through the half-open window. She shook her head.

"Good for you," said Jimmy. "These things'll stunt your growth." He laughed, a burst of noise. "I should know."

Portia waited until he'd lit his cigarette before she asked, "What did you mean back there? About me never begging for anything?" The smoke was going right into her eyes, but she didn't move to wave it away.

"I seen girls like you before. Every year they show up on the lot, looking for work, looking for something different than what they come from. They never last long."

Rain clouds were beginning to roll across the sky. Portia crossed her arms against the sudden breeze. "I'm no First o'May."

If he was surprised by her easy use of the phrase, he didn't show it. "Like I said" — Jimmy exhaled a lungful of smoke in her direction — "I seen it before."

She wasn't going to win him over here and now, and it was getting chilly. She could smell the rain on the air. *Can't afford to catch cold,* she thought. *Might lose my voice. Jackal would kill me.*

"You're probably right," said Portia.

"I usually am," said Jimmy.

"So I guess we should say our goodbyes now. Get it out of the way."

He raised a thick eyebrow.

"It's been real nice working with you, Jimmy." She put her hand through the window again, in handshake position.

He regarded her hand as if it were a venomous snake. Then, slowly, he switched his cigarette from his right hand to his left and put his palm against hers. It was surprisingly warm, and soft. *Not a hand that's done a lot of work. Not like Mosco's, or Gideon's.*

She gripped Jimmy's hand for a moment — a moment just long enough to seal a secret, or a promise — and then she let go and walked back to the midway, leaving him alone, the way he always said he wanted to be.

Jimmy

First time I heard her name, sounded like Gideon said, "Portion," and I thought, *What the hell kinda name is that?*

She's probably just like everybody else from the outside. Thinks I should be happy and cute because I'm small. Goddamned cartoon movie about that girl and the seven dwarfs practically ruined my life. You'd think everybody in America saw that damned movie. Maybe they did. All I know is people see me now and they want me to sing that goddamned "heigh-ho" song, and no way in hell am I gonna do that. Humiliating enough having Jim carry me around like some kinda baby.

He means well, Jim does. And I do hate slogging through the mud. Takes me forever to get anywhere when the mud's up.

I like summer on the open road 'cause there ain't a lotta mud to deal with. Seems like it's always dry out here and I can walk across a field like anybody else. Grass gets tall on the prairie, taller than me by far, and I just tie a scarf around my face and put some sunglasses on so the weeds don't whack me in the eyes, and then I can walk as far as I want.

Anyway, I still think Portia's a weird name. And she can go to hell if she thinks I'm singin' that song for her.

JIM

Sometimes it feels like I've always been this tall. I can't remember ever being shorter than anyone else, having to tilt my head back to see a face or stand on my tiptoes to reach something. I can reach everything. I hate going to the grocery store the most because there's always some smart-mouthed fellow who wants to give his friends a laugh so he asks me if I can get something off the top shelf for him. Of course I can. The top shelf isn't even as high as my chest. Anyone can see that.

I see mothers on the midway, holding their little boys and girls, and I wonder what it would be like to have somebody hold me like that. I asked Jimmy what it feels like when I hold him, but he told me I was being strange again. I guess I understand—I mean, Jimmy doesn't want to think of himself being like a baby.

Sometimes I wish there was a magician who really could saw people in half. But I wouldn't really want to give up half of myself. (It'd have to be the bottom half, I guess, because I couldn't likely go on living without a head.) What I really wish is that someone could melt me and Jimmy together and make us into two normal-size people. I'd even settle for being attached to each other like Pippa and Polly are. I wouldn't mind.

But I don't think Jimmy wants to talk about being melted down with me or attached so we'd have to always be in the same place. I think Jimmy kind of likes being small, sometimes. I don't mind carrying him around when the mud gets bad, and he ties my shoes for me.

It's too hard for me to bend over anymore, so I can't do it myself.

How's that for irony? I can reach just about anything, except the ground.

Life sure is strange.

The Secret Lives of Ladies

Do me a favor," Violet said. "Take this plate to Mrs. Collington. She didn't show up to dinner."

"Maybe she wasn't hungry," said Portia.

"Yeah, right," Violet retorted. "Anyway, Mosco doesn't like her to skip meals. She loses any weight, and he loses money."

Mrs. Collington didn't appear to be in any danger of losing her Fat Lady title, even if she skipped dinner for a week, but Portia took the plate (which really was more of a platter, loaded with fried chicken and biscuits) and headed for the trailer.

Unlike some of the freaks, Mrs. Collington didn't have a trailer with her name and image painted on the outside in garish colors. The Lucasie trailer, for instance, was visible from miles away—larger-than-life portraits of Rudolph and Antoinette and Joseph under huge red print that said THE WILD ALBINOS OF BORA BORA and slightly smaller print (but only slightly) that said THE AMAZING LUCASIE FAMILY. Next to Joseph was a curiously solid swatch of red, as if he were being overlapped by an enormous curtain.

"That used to be me," Violet had told Portia when she asked about it. "I made them paint over it."

Mrs. Collington's trailer, though, was a plain silver Airstream with a plain silver door with a small rectangle painted on it, which simply said COLLINGTON. No one passing by would have known who lived there. Probably, Portia thought, that was the point.

She knocked gently and nearly dropped the platter when Mrs. Murphy threw the door open and thrust her bearded face into the cool evening air.

"Hello, dear! Gosh, it's nice out, isn't it? Is that for us? Come in!"

Mrs. Murphy held the door, and Portia felt the woman's beard tickle her neck as she stepped inside. Mrs. Collington was spread across the couches at the far end.

"Violet sent me with your dinner," Portia said.

"Look at all this," Mrs. Murphy said, shaking her head. "They always send too much."

"I'm not hungry," Mrs. Collington called. "You eat it."

Mrs. Murphy leaned close to Portia and whispered, "She gets depressed sometimes, and then she gets stubborn. Decides she's going to quit the business. It happens every year around this time."

"Why?" Portia whispered.

"Her wedding anniversary."

"Stop talking about me like I'm not here," Mrs. Collington snapped. "You can't keep secrets in a trailer this size. And I'm not depressed."

"You're not? Well, good, then. Let's all have some dinner."

"Oh," said Portia, "I've already eaten."

"Nonsense," Mrs. Murphy said. She took the platter and went to join Mrs. Collington in the living room. "Come on," she called, and patted the seat next to her. "Come tell us about yourself."

Portia froze. She had grown accustomed to keeping her secrets—no one but Gideon knew anything about her past, and even he didn't know the most important part. *Caroline.* Portia shook her head.

"I'm sure you have much more interesting stories than I do," she ventured.

"See?" Mrs. Murphy elbowed Mrs. Collington. "I told you. She's just like Gideon."

"What do you mean?"

"He changes the subject whenever you ask him anything personal. Tries to get you talking about yourself instead of him. Fortunately for you"—Mrs. Murphy winked at Portia—"I am always delighted to talk about myself. And so is Mrs. Collington. Usually."

"Knock it off and pass the chicken, Emmeline."

"Breast or drumstick, Fern?"

"Both," said Mrs. Collington. "Thank you, *dear.*"

"You're welcome, *darling.*"

They sounded like sisters, teasing each other with niggling pet names and exaggerated good manners. Manners layered over a pair of roughened hearts that loved each other.

"So," Mrs. Murphy said, "where shall I begin?"

"At the beginning," Portia told her, and accepted a biscuit from the plate Mrs. Collington had extended across the table.

The two women proceeded to speak for what felt like hours. Portia's entire childhood had been just like this, letting her ears fill with the sounds of familiar voices speaking remembrances of past lives and long-gone people, the smell of food heavy in the air, the words flying like insects, buzzing, swarming, dancing. She found herself lulled into a strange kind of trance, her body relaxing for the first time since she could remember.

She felt safe.

But then the chicken and the biscuits were gone, and a new silence fell over the women at the table. Suddenly, Mrs. Murphy's hands flew to her chest, clasping her splendid beard. "Oh!" she cried. "The dress!"

Mrs. Collington leaned back on the couch, which groaned deeply. "What dress?" she inquired in a contented voice.

"The dress for Portia! Stand up, dear. Let me measure you. Now, where did I put that sewing box?" She bustled around the tiny room, digging through drawers and various piles of objects until she found her quarry: a rusty silver lunch box. Max had had one just like it. Portia swallowed.

"You don't have to —" she started, but Mrs. Murphy waved her objections away.

"Of course I do, dear," she said. "It's my great pleasure! Arms up."

If it had been years since Portia had sat and listened to so many stories, it had been an entire lifetime since she'd been made to stand still for so long, and even longer, it seemed, since anyone had sought any kind of physical contact. Mrs. Murphy's tape measure gently recorded every bit of Portia's body — Mrs. Collington wrote its findings down on a slip of paper as Mrs. Murphy reported each number. Portia could not have felt more exposed than if she'd confessed every sin she'd ever committed, and yet the experience was far from unpleasant. She liked the sight of the numbers on the paper, when she looked at them later. They were, she thought, a kind of proof of her residence in the world.

It was nice to know that this was not all just a dream.

"Tell Jackal I'll have it ready in a week or so," Mrs. Murphy called as Portia departed, empty platter in hand. "You'll look just lovely, dear!"

Portia smiled, waved, and let the midway carry her off.

Mrs. Collington

Been billed as everything from a giant baby to a dancing girl. Had my hair blond, black, red, long, short, gone. You name it. Mosco don't go for gimmicks like the others. He's smarter than that. He only lets the twins do their dancing 'cause they're so spoiled. The rest of us mostly just stay in one place and don't make too much eye contact. Rubes wanna get a good look at you but they don't always want you looking back.

I usually got a big smile on my face, and I wave like I'm a beauty queen on a parade float so they get the whole jolly-and-fat combination. But I ain't really looking at anybody. I fix my eyes on a spot a couple inches over all their heads and pretend.

They did love the giant baby routine, once upon a time. I was just a kid then, six or seven years old. I already weighed over a hundred pounds. My giant baby diaper was the size of a curtain, and my giant baby bonnet had extra-long ribbons so I could tie it in a bow under my chins. And this other girl, Mamie or Millie or something, played my mama and fed me and burped me, and I sat on her lap and she acted like I was crushing her.

Only, a couple times I really did give her bruises on her legs.

And it was near impossible to drink outta that giant baby bottle without getting milk all over us.

I can't stand milk anymore. Haven't had it in years.

Sitting in one place for so long, a person can start to go a little crazy. Not the kind of crazy you don't come back from. Just a few steps in the direction of not-all-there. Once, I swear, I saw an eye through a knothole in the stage. Right at my feet. It was looking at me. It didn't blink. Or maybe it blinked at the exact same time I blinked, so I tried not blinking, but I couldn't help it. Then Mrs. Murphy asked me what was wrong because I was looking down instead of smiling and waving like usual, and I told her I was just tired, and when I looked at the knothole again, the eye was gone.

I try not to think about things like that. Cooking helps. Eating, too.

Good thing I'm in the business.

THE MEANING OF "I DON'T KNOW"

Between working in the pie car and trying to absorb Jackal's vast collection of instructions on How to Get a Man's Last Dollar, Portia was exhausted. Each day seemed like a replica of the day before. She did not even feel like riding her bicycle, which sat in the back of Gideon's truck when the show traveled, and otherwise leaned dejectedly against Portia and Violet's trailer. She desperately wanted to leave the pie car and never set foot into a kitchen again. The freaks were an ungrateful audience for her work. It was like cooking for a brood of cranky children, none of whom liked the same things or wanted to try anything new.

"Mashed potatoes again?"

"Scrambled eggs again?"

"This looks . . . interesting."

"How come we never have watermelon anymore?"

Joseph said, "I'm sick of chicken legs."

Jimmy said, "This is bullshit."

"Jimmy!" everyone hollered.

"Well it is," he muttered.

Portia gritted her teeth. She made every recipe she could

think of. At least the ones that were possible, given the meager ingredients she had to work with. Shopping trips were discouraged — Mosco saw every trip into town as a potential disaster, and money was scarce — so Portia and Violet were often dispatched to barter with local farmers and housewives in exchange for circus tickets. They never mentioned the sideshow.

Portia did not complain. She thought about how she could be shoveling horse manure instead and went on peeling the seventeen-thousandth potato she had peeled that summer. She had visions of herself peeling potatoes until the end of the world, at which point she would perish alone because no one would be able to find her amid all the naked potatoes and piles of shredded skins.

But the day after she took the platter of chicken and biscuits to Mrs. Collington's trailer, the Fat and Bearded Ladies whirled into the kitchen and ordered Portia to leave immediately.

"What? Why?"

Mrs. Collington tightened her mouth and said simply, "Out."

Mrs. Murphy smiled as she tied a scarf over her beard. "She's feeling better," she whispered to Portia. "Now hand me that peeler."

Mosco was outside the pie car, whittling chess pieces out of discarded stage boards.

"Who're those for?" Portia asked.

Mosco muttered, "I don't know."

She waited a few seconds, but he said nothing more.

"Well . . . I guess I'll . . . take a bath?"

Eyes still down, he said, "You asking my opinion?"

"Just trying to make conversation."

He looked up then and closed his pocketknife. "Let me give you some advice. And I'm only doing this because it looks like you might actually stick around awhile. In the carnival, when you ask a question and the answer you get is 'I don't know,' it means you have crossed a line. It means, 'None of your business.' It means you are not entitled to know something just because you ask about it. Understand?"

"Yes."

"Good," he said. "Now leave me alone. I've got to finish this in time for Marie's birthday. And if you tell anyone I told you what I just told you, you're fired."

Portia wasn't sure what he meant was the secret: the business about "I don't know" or the fact that he was carving a chess set for Marie. But Portia had just been set free from the pie car and threatened with unemployment, all in the span of about three minutes. Her future at the Wonder Show was no more secure than a bridge made of eggshells. She wasn't about to disagree with the boss.

"Right," she said. And that was that.

THE LEGEND OF MARIE

Mosco was the strongman, the mighty fellow who nonchalantly bent iron bars to look like wishbones, let Jackal snap his wrists into shackles so he could break the chains with a satisfying pop, silently lifted a barbell with two children from the audience sitting on either end. He did not smile or grimace or try to look mean. He simply did what was necessary, finished his portion of the show, and returned to his business.

Of course it had occurred to him to hire another strongman and spare himself the inconvenience of performing, but the only thing more bothersome than doing the shows would have been paying someone else to do them. He was capable. And the exercise was good for him.

And it gave him an excuse to be standing front and center when Marie took the stage. As the plucky opening strains of Josephine Baker's *La Petite Tonkinoise* wafted out of the speakers above the stage, Marie stepped gracefully from behind the curtain and took her position. As if in a dream, Mosco watched as Marie stood on one leg and brought the other foot to the small wooden table at her side, selected a knife, gripped it between her toes, and fired it at the target with perfect accuracy.

Then, with the thud of the knife piercing wood, a shudder went through the crowd like a chill wind through tall grass. It was the precise moment when the spectacle became real, when they realized what was before their eyes: a beautiful, deadly, disfigured creature. Marie, the Armless Knife-Thrower.

Anna appeared at the other end of the platform, removed the knives from the target, replaced them on the table, and returned to stand with her back pressed against the target.

Marie could make a knife do anything. Pin a fly to the wall, cut an apple in perfect halves, cut a lock of her sister's hair without ever drawing blood.

But she didn't do her best tricks anymore. The only thing worse than being poor, she said, was being famous. That's when you stopped being a real person. People told stories about you, and the stories got bigger until you were more in their eyes than you could ever be in your own. They took your soul that way.

So she did enough to stay well known, enough to keep Anna in good clothes and herself in sharp blades, and tried to forget about the rest.

Except some nights, every now and then, she let it roll back to her like water coming through a dry riverbed. She tucked her head through her leather sash and let it fall around her neck, walked to a stand of trees or an empty building, and threw knives in the moonlight. She did it by feel, by the position of her leg and the strength of the wind (if there was any). She did it by sound. By instinct. By magic, almost.

It was there, in her own quiet country, that Marie was truly happy.

Her costume was dark blue satin, like a layer of the ocean

no one had ever seen. It had a halter neckline because she liked to show off her perfect shoulders, below which there might have been a pair of perfect arms except that she'd been born without them. She was not ashamed of the emptiness along the sides of her body. In fact, she couldn't imagine having limbs there — how unwieldy they would be, dangling there, waving around, whatever arms might do. She did not mourn the lack of them. She simply did not need them.

Marie could sign her name, comb her hair, clean her kitchen, turn the pages of a book as delicately as if her toes were fingers. When she spoke, she sat down and crossed her legs and gestured emphatically with her upper foot.

And of course, she could throw a knife with unflinching accuracy.

"Show me how you do it," Portia begged. She had watched Marie's show a dozen times by then and still couldn't figure out how the knives went from Marie's toes to the standing target board at the other end of the stage. It happened too quickly. There was Marie standing like a crane, poised on one foot with the other leg raised, holding a knife between her toes, and then she gave a little kick and the knife was in the target. She made it look easy, but Portia had tried to mimic the motion (knife free, because she didn't want to cut anyone, especially herself) and felt nothing but awkward.

Marie shrugged her orphaned shoulders. "You can watch me rehearse, if you like. But I cannot throw the knives any slower. You must watch more closely."

"How did you learn to do it, though? Do you remember when you started?"

Marie ignored the question. She raised a slippered foot and

pointed to the thick roll of felt waiting on the steps of her trailer. "You can carry my knives for me. Anna has gone into town."

"How'd she get Mosco to let her?"

Marie shrugged again. "She is quiet, my sister, but she is persuasive."

Portia grabbed the bundle, and they walked the short distance to the midway stage.

Marie used her toes to hold the back of her shoe and lifted her heel out, first the left and then the right. She wiggled her bare toes in the grass. "I was very small when I began. My father taught me—he was a knife-thrower in the old days. He quit when he met my mother, but he never forgot the art."

The word *father* made Portia swallow hard. "Did he use his feet, too?"

"You're asking me if he had arms."

"Yes."

"He did. But he tied his hands behind his back so he could teach me to throw with my feet. We learned together that way."

"Did he teach Anna?"

"No. She was normal." Marie rolled her head side to side, to loosen up and make sure her sister wasn't nearby. "She *is* normal. She can do other things. She did not need to learn the art."

"That doesn't mean she wouldn't want to know how to do it," Portia said.

Marie mounted the steps, walked to her mark, and tapped the stage with her toe. "The knives, please."

Portia ran up and set the bundle down at Marie's feet. She untied the ribbon that secured it and unrolled the felt, revealing the long row of knife handles. The blades were concealed in deep pockets that were sewn to fit each knife like a tailored sleeve. Aunt Sophia had the same kind of case for her knitting needles. She had made it herself.

Portia wondered who had made this one for Marie.

Before she could ask, Marie waved her away with the flick of a foot and started to slide the knives out of their pockets. Not all the way, just enough so that she could grip the base of each blade with her toes and lift the knife into position.

"It is important," said Marie, "to have each knife in the same place each time, because each knife is different. So each throw is different. If I throw the fourth knife just the way I throw the third, the pattern will be ruined."

Portia had the beginning of a thought, the image of Anna posed against the target board and a knife thrown the wrong way. She shook it away and concentrated on the chain of motions Marie created with her throwing leg. Her right leg, closest to the edge of the stage, closest to the audience.

She could throw with her left just as well, but if the crowd couldn't see the whole sequence, it simply wasn't as impressive. And above all, Marie was a performer.

"It is quite simple. A combination of heart and precision."

"That's what Aunt Sophia used to say about baking," said Portia.

"Was she right?" asked Marie.

"Sometimes," said Portia. "But not always."

FROM THE NOTEBOOK OF PORTIA REMINI

Once upon a time
I made an apple tree
It grew too tall to climb
It shadowed over me

On every reaching limb
The apple blossoms flowered
But when the fruit came in
The apples all were sour

Once upon a time
When promises were made
The stories all were mine
But now the stories fade.

FAMILY RECIPE

In her notebook, Portia wrote stories told by other people, rhymes a child might sing, bits of conversation she overheard on the midway, descriptions of the rubes that processed through the tent every evening like ghosts. She tried to be watchful, and to see every face, and she kept a tally of how many men she saw who could have been Max but weren't. Each one was a bit wrong in some way—too short, too old, too young, loud, cruel, sad, heavy, dark. Looking so closely at strangers gave Portia the sensation of wearing spectacles that distorted everyone just slightly. She began to wonder if the sideshow tent actually changed people, as if upon entering they were rendered different by one degree.

The only folks who looked right were the ones on stage.

Every night, after the bally was done and the crowds had dispersed from the last circus show, as the roustabouts broke down the lot and prepared to get back on the road, Portia huddled in her trailer and scribbled words onto paper, hoping they would mean something, make something happen.

How many more days could she tell herself *one more day*? This had been her only plan. She was immobilized by the possibility that it simply would not work. Worse, Gideon seemed to have adopted her search for Max as a personal cause. Perhaps to make up for having teased her about the bicycle, or for reasons of his own that he did not decide to share, he hounded her daily about her progress.

"See him?" he'd ask. "Anything?"

"No," she mumbled.

Having to say aloud over and over that she had not found Max, nor anyone who even closely resembled him, made Portia furious. She did her best not to show it — her temper had gotten the best of her before. But this time, she lost her resolve.

"Leave me alone!"

Gideon looked as if he'd been slapped. His hands sank into his pockets, and he let his breath out slowly. Then he said, "I put up a sign in the ticket window with his name on it, saying he's got free tickets waiting for him. Word could get around that way."

Portia blinked. "How do you do that?" she asked.

"Do what?"

"Just . . . breathe like that. Stay so calm. How do you do it?"

He smiled, drew his hands out, spread them in front of her. "Magic," he said, and began whistling like a calliope.

Portia laughed. It sounded strange to her, her voice bending to that cadence. Gideon smiled again.

"You'll find him," he told her.

She knew he was only trying to make her feel better. There was no reason to believe in Max showing up on the lot, no mysterious force that kept fathers and daughters in the same universe simply because their blood was the same recipe. And yet, as Portia looked around, at the dusky sky and the great flat expanse of prairie and the bones of the circus readied for their journey, she thought she could feel something—a buoyancy, a lifting of the ground under her feet, keeping her upright. Perhaps this was the physics of faith, the knowledge that the earth was moving and so was she.

"Thank you," Portia said.

And she continued to spin.

More Secrets

Each week was a cycle, built out of scheduled tasks that no one ignored or questioned. Bathe on Monday, wash clothes on Tuesday, go to the market on Wednesday, clean house on Thursday, mend costumes and canvas on Friday. Extra shows on Saturday. Day off on Sunday. For the circus performers and the human marvels (plus Jackal and Portia), every day brought rehearsal, and for the roustabouts and mechanics there were constant repairs, and the near-daily breakdown, transport, and reassembly of the circus. But that was work. The rituals of regular life happened one day at a time, each week, like a wheel in perpetual motion.

The circus and the Wonder Show followed the same schedule, but the circus people did certain things first. There was only so much space in the dining tent and only so many washtubs and only so many stalls in the bank of outdoor showers, so the carnival folks ate second, washed their clothes second, bathed second. They were accustomed to eating warm food instead of hot or cold, to bathing under high noon sun instead of low morning light, to wearing clothes that were never quite as clean as they might have liked.

Portia, though, had gotten used to the privileges of living in Mister's house (dubious as they were). And she did not appreciate having to wait around for the seemingly endless trail of circus performers to finish eating or bathing or washing their clothes before she could do the same.

She and Violet were sitting in the ancient lawn chairs, watching the sun climb the sky and waiting for their chance to clean up. Portia felt especially filthy — it had been almost two weeks since her escape from Mister, and she'd had only one real bath. Most days she had to be satisfied with a bowl of lukewarm water and one of Jackal's handkerchiefs. The trailer she was sharing with Violet was, to put it kindly, a classic model. No running water, no electricity, and no bathroom. Some of the better-known circus performers had new Airstream trailers with all sorts of modern luxuries (or so Violet said), and Portia glared at their gleaming steel skins with all the envy she could muster. But it was too hot even for that.

"This is ridiculous," Violet said irritably. "I swear it takes longer and longer every week for them to get finished. What are they, showering the horses, too?"

"At least we get to go first after they're done. It's nice of Mosco to set it up that way."

"Nice, nothing. If the men went first, Mrs. Murphy and Mrs. Collington'd likely string him up by his belt loops and leave him for dead."

The rest of the women paced nearby — Mrs. Murphy, Mrs. Collington, Mrs. Lucasie, Anna, Marie . . .

"Where's Doula?" Portia asked. "And the twins?"

Violet shrugged. "They usually go to a hotel in town. The

twins make enough money from the blowoff to get a room for a few hours, and Doula goes with them. To help them, I guess."

"What's the blowoff?"

Violet lowered her sunglasses. "Jackal hasn't told you?"

Portia shook her head, and Violet sat up in her chair and leaned forward. She was suddenly crackling with energy.

"Remember what I said about the ten-in-one? How this used to be a real show?"

Portia noticed Mrs. Murphy squinting in her direction and hoped she couldn't hear what Violet was saying. It felt a little rude to be gossiping with everyone so nearby. Violet, however, wasn't bothered.

"Well, without The Human Torso, the two big draws are Marie and the twins. So Pippa decided she and Polly should do something different, something more interesting, to draw the crowds. She got Mosco to let her and Polly start a new act on the back stage."

Behind the curtain Jackal had refused to let her pass through.

"What kind of act?"

Violet leaned closer. "They dance."

"So?"

"Naked."

Portia's face blushed hot, and for some reason she thought of Caroline. *She would have been horrified,* Portia told herself. *And I would have told her she was silly for it.*

"Are you all right?" Violet asked.

Portia fanned herself with one of Violet's movie magazines. "I'm fine," she said.

"Maybe I shouldn't have told you."

"I was bound to find out sometime," said Portia. "Anyway, there are worse things in the world than dancing girls."

Men without remorse. Families who leave their little girls behind in dark places.

"I suppose there are," said Violet. "Anyway, you should see it. The act. Especially if you're supposed to be the inside talker."

"Jackal won't let me in."

"I'll get you in," said Violet, determination in her voice. "Done it before."

Then it was their turn for the shower, and suddenly Portia felt self-conscious, as if talking about Polly and Pippa's being naked had changed what being naked meant. She tried to imagine the feeling of it, on stage, with an audience looking at her. Men, looking at her.

She finished her shower and dressed quickly, wanting to be covered, not caring if her clothes stuck to her still-damp skin.

Mosco

Look, I've been on this circuit a long time. My whole life, maybe. I can't remember anything other than this, so it might be my whole life or it might just be I can't remember anything else.

I always knew I'd have my own show and it would be a respectable operation. No pickled punks or monkeys turned into mermaids. No pinheads. No naked girls.

But sometimes a man has to make concessions. There's certain things the rubes want to see, and the twins, they wore me down. I love those girls like they were my own, and I never wanted 'em jiggling around in front of a crowd full of perverts, but they wore me down. They know the game. They're either on the regular stage getting the same pay as everybody else, or they're the blowoff. Hell of a lot more money in the blowoff. And you can't have a blowoff that's tame. They know that.

I protect them. That's all I can do. I'm next to the stage at every performance, and those guys in the crowd have already seen me outside. They've seen me bend a steel pipe in half. They won't mess with the twins while I'm there.

That's all I can do.

Still.

I don't ever look.

POLLY

Sometimes me and Pippa get to meet other twins when we go to new places. Never twins like us, y'know, attached like us, but still it's nice to talk to them. These girls from Biloxi said sometimes they have the exact same dreams, just like me and Pippa. And they had a secret language, too, like we used to have. I guess we grew out of it, though.

People think we must be just alike, me and Pippa, but we're not. She's smarter than me, and she reads more books than me. I learned how to knit so I'd have something to do when she's reading. I'm pretty good at it now, but I still get bored. I guess I'm lucky I'm on the left, because I can do all the driving and Pippa can read while we're on the road. I think I'd go crazy if I couldn't drive.

I know we're real lucky, too, because we each have two arms we can use and two legs, too. We heard about some twin boys from Italy who only had two legs between them but they had separate top halves and they couldn't even walk. They had to crawl around on the floor like babies. That would be awful. I think Pippa would hate me even more if we were like that.

She says she doesn't hate me at all, but she's the one who always talks about if we were different. I don't even like to imagine if we were different. I would miss her so much. And if we were born like this, doesn't that mean God made us this way for a reason? I don't even say that to Pippa anymore, though, because she says she doesn't believe in God, and that makes me upset. The preacher said those who don't believe will go straight to hell.

I would rather go to hell with Pippa than be in heaven without her. I wonder if we could go in two different directions when we're dead.

Pippa was the one who got us started dancing for the blow-off. Before that we were on the stage with everybody else, and I liked that fine, but Pippa wanted to make more money so we could save up for a house someday. She talks a lot about our house and how it'll have a huge room full of books so she can read all the time.

I don't know what I'll do then.

Lots more knitting, I guess.

PIPPA

I don't know if Polly and I would be friends in other circumstances. I don't know if we're friends now. I take care of her and I take care of myself, and that would probably be true if we were just regular sisters. Maybe it seems funny to talk about it that way when we're up on stage, dancing like loose women do, but that is how I see it. One does what is necessary to survive.

Mr. Charles Darwin wrote about survival and the ways in which creatures evolve to keep their places in the world. I certainly do not think Polly and I are a good example of evolution—if every person was born with another person attached to them, many scientific and technical advances would be rendered useless. The airplane, for example, would have to be completely redesigned. Think if the Wright brothers had been like us. Or Cain and Abel. Human history could have changed direction at so many crossroads.

As an example of survival, however, Polly and I have done admirably. And we have been in good company here. What is a man with alligator skin going to do besides make a performer of himself? For most of us, it is this life or one spent hiding in a dark corner somewhere. An institution or an alley, it makes no difference.

But I am not content to settle for mere survival. I require a greater measure of success. I believe I have made this clear to Polly (as clear as I am able) and, in another way, to Mosco. He was reluctant to allow us to dance, but I promised him that we would have no trouble finding another home and reminded him that his previous exhibit of Siamese twins was lacking in authenticity, being merely two girls who looked alike wearing a pair of dresses that had been sewn together. Mosco is a savvy businessman. He came around to my way of thinking.

Polly does not enjoy the dancing and neither do I, but I talk the both of us onto the stage every night. I talk about the money we are saving from our ticket sales, about the house we will buy, about the bookshelves that will line the walls and the fireplace that will keep us warm on winter nights. And I promise Polly as much yarn as she could ever want.

THE BLOWOFF

Extra canvas was layered over the gaps in this part of the tent, to help the rubes forget the midway and the eyes that would judge them silently for paying the extra dollar, for what they were about to watch. A single spotlight exhaled a dim beam onto the stage. The rows of chairs sat in almost total darkness, and the men stumbled as they walked in. Mosco liked this arrangement, liked how it made the rubes less confident, less likely to put on a show of their own by jumping the stage or shouting lewd suggestions. Just the same, he took his place at the stage corner, set his stance, and crossed his arms. The men were silent.

Portia and Violet made their way to a pair of seats in the back and tried to stay out of sight. The shadowed heads in front of them were, Portia thought, like the shadows she saw filling the trucks at night when the show pulled up stakes and moved on to the next town. The comparison wouldn't sit still in her brain, though she knew there was a difference. Her friends were not like these men. They were the spectacle, not the spectators. They had done nothing wrong. Only what they *had* to do, to survive.

But if that was the case, Polly and Pippa could have been on the stage with the others instead of singled out for the blowoff. Couldn't they?

They danced to Fred Astaire singing "Cheek to Cheek," touching their faces and then pivoting so their backs were to the audience. Then they each lifted a side of their skirt to reveal the band of flesh that joined them at their shapely hips. When Fred sang, "I want my arms about you," the twins embraced and grinned lasciviously, hinting at other, less innocent embraces. And at the last chorus, they reached across each other's bodies and tore away the tops of their costumes, and the men howled and barked, and Portia finally looked away.

IMPRESSIONS

"I'll tell you a secret," Violet said.

Portia wasn't sure she wanted another secret to carry, but she nodded anyway.

"Doula's not really a gypsy. Or a fortuneteller. She's just some old woman from Greece."

"How do you know she can't tell fortunes?"

"I took her some tea leaves to read once, and she didn't know how to do it. I showed her the cup and asked her what it meant, and she said"—Violet hunched herself over and spoke in Doula's deep graveled voice—"'Means you need more tea.'"

Portia laughed. "Well, she wasn't exactly wrong."

Violet hopped forward in a perfect imitation of Doula's lurching walk and hollered, "I am Doula! I tell you the future if you give me the vodka!"

"Violet," Portia hissed. "She'll hear you."

"I can imitate anyone here. Watch." Violet made herself squat and bowlegged and waved an invisible hat around. "Goddammit!"

"Jimmy!"

"Right. I can do everyone, I'm telling you."

"Do Gideon."

Violet looked at her blankly. "Gideon?"

"You said you can imitate anyone."

"I can. But Gideon's not . . ."

"What?"

"He's just normal."

"I thought you liked normal."

"I do. But normal doesn't make for much of a show." Violet sighed and climbed back into her lost-and-found chair. "Not around here, anyway."

Trouble Inside

She was getting used to it, working on the inside. It wasn't like Jackal had said it would be. The show he described had existed once, maybe, but now it was different. Rubes weren't rubes anymore. They didn't believe in what they saw, they all thought they knew the truth, and they weren't shy about theorizing how the tricks were pulled. Loudly.

"No way that fella's eight feet tall!"

"Beard's fake. You can see the glue!"

"No such thing as albinos, everyone knows that. Buncha coloreds in white makeup, all that is."

And so on. Portia did her best to preserve order in the tent, not wanting to get Jackal involved, not wanting to ask for a rescue. Mrs. Collington and the others did their best, too, to maintain their composure and their distance. But sometimes the temptation to shout back was too much to resist, and then Mosco would appear to silently escort the offending parties from the show. Refunds sometimes had to be provided, to avoid further trouble. None of it was good for business.

Today's crowd, Portia was relieved to see, looked remarkably well behaved. It was brutally hot, which made people cranky but also meant they lacked the energy to get themselves really riled up. The air coated everyone like an extra skin. Portia's white dress stuck to her legs when she walked into the tent, leading her small group of expectant spectators like ducklings across a road. There were a handful of folks from town, an older man in a suit who kept whispering to a group of five young men as they scribbled in small notebooks, and a quartet of soldiers, stiff and silent in their uniforms. One of them had his left cuff pinned up to his shoulder, the empty sleeve creased where his elbow had once resided. Portia had seen him watching Marie as she threw her knives, his face somber, his posture perfectly straight.

As the group made its way into the tent, Portia took her place at the far end of the stage and was just about to begin her bally when the older gentleman began to speak. He looked only at his companions, but everyone had become his audience.

"Here," he said, "we find a classic assortment of so-called freaks, who display a range of medical issues." He waved a hand casually toward Mrs. Collington. "Thyroid!" he crowed.

The young men nodded and wrote furiously in their notebooks.

The older man jabbed a finger at the Lucasies. "Garden variety albinism!"

"I beg your pardon," Mr. Lucasie started to say, but his accuser had already moved on to Jim.

"Here we have a clear case of acromegalic gigantism," the man declared. "Most often caused by a benign tumor on the pituitary gland. Problem is, the internal organs grow right along with the skeletal frame. That's probably what will kill him, in the end."

Jim looked stricken. Portia felt she should say something, but suddenly felt ridiculous in her lily white dress and her braids tied with ribbons. She felt like a little girl playing dress-up. She hoped Mosco could hear them — she wondered if she should fetch him, but she was afraid to leave, to call attention to herself.

"How old are you, son?" the man asked Jim.

Jim stammered, "Nineteen, sir."

"Don't tell him that!" Jimmy snapped. "None of his damned business how old you are, or anything else. Sonofabitch."

The man ignored Jimmy completely. "How tall are you?"

"I'm not sure, sir," Jim confessed. "It's been a long time since anyone measured me."

"But you're still growing?"

"Yes, I think so."

Jimmy slammed his foot into Jim's shin. "Shut the hell up, would you?" he howled. "What does this guy know, anyway?"

"I happen to be a medical doctor and an expert on glandular disorders," the man replied calmly. "And I can tell you that your friend's condition could be easily remedied with surgical means."

"You mean," said Jim, "I could be normal?"

The word ricocheted like a bullet around the tent, hitting everyone at once. Jim immediately realized what he'd said and clapped a huge hand over his mouth. But it was too late to retrieve it.

If the doctor noticed the sudden weight of the silence that fell upon them, he did not acknowledge it. Instead, he said, "If your condition is caused by a tumor, and the tumor was removed, you would stop growing. But not right away. It could take several years for your growth to slow, and it might already be too late if your heart and your liver are grossly enlarged."

"Oh," Jim said.

The doctor's students had stopped writing. They all looked at Jim with practiced sympathy, as if they were rehearsing a scene in a play in which a patient receives bad news.

"I think that's enough for one day," the doctor said, and he led his followers out of the entrance before Portia had a chance to direct them to the back exit. She knew Polly and Pippa were waiting in the tent's shadowy annex, but she doubted anyone in the sparse, dejected crowd would be interested in paying an extra dollar today.

"Ladies and gentlemen," she said, "you may exit this way."

As they did so, the soldier with one arm stopped in front of Jim. "Doctors," he spat. "They think they know everything."

"Right," Jim replied, his deep, throaty voice barely audible.

"Let me tell you," the soldier said, "there ain't nothing easy about surgery. And all doctors want to talk about is how much better your life will be after you let 'em cut you apart. Don't you listen, son. Don't you listen to a word of it."

Jim smiled weakly. "I won't."

"All right then," the soldier said, and he followed his friends back to the midway, back to the outside where the heat and the sun waited to assault them once more.

VIOLET

I don't hate my family. I've tried, believe me. But I always end up feeling guilty because why should I hate them when they're the ones who have to live this way, trapped inside all day because they can't even go out in the sun?

That's why they work under that extra layer of canvas—they have a tent within a tent just in case some sunlight gets through.

They will never be part of the world.

I'm afraid I won't either. Even though I can be outside without dark glasses and a floppy hat like Mama's. Even though I can walk the midway without anyone staring at me, eat a hot dog, ride an elephant. Mr. Bishop let me do that once, and I waved to all these kids who were watching and they waved back.

Because I am normal.

They didn't know that after I got off the elephant, I had to go make new curtains for the trailer because the old moth-bitten ones let the sun in. They didn't know that I had to make the stupid curtains because no one else in my family can see well enough to sew. Or clean. Or read. Or drive. Which is why Jackal used to drive our truck until I turned ten, and then I drove, sitting on Papa's lap and telling him, "Gas. Brake. Gas. Slow down. Faster." Until I could reach the pedals and then I drove by myself and Papa sat in the back with Mama and Joseph.

A few months ago I gave the keys back to Jackal. Started riding in my own trailer, trying to sleep at night like regular folks.

I will never tell Papa I missed him when I was driving.

I will never get married in a field of wildflowers, unless it's in the middle of the night.

I will never be free.

Unless I'm alone.

JOSEPH

When Mother and Father argue, which isn't very often, it is always about me. Mother says, "Rudolph, he is only a child," and Father says, "What does that have to do with anything?" and I agree with Father. Mother is not wrong about my age, but she is wrong about what it means.

Which is to say, it means nothing.

We sit on the stage all together, except for Violet because she is nothing much to look at. Plus she hates it. The first show we worked for, they tried to get Violet up there with us because they wanted everyone to see how weird it was that one person in a family could be so different than the rest. But Violet wouldn't go and Mother and Father didn't make her because they feel guilty about her.

They don't feel guilty about me, though. I am just what they always wanted.

I have never told anyone this before, but sometimes I feel sorry for Violet. She isn't special like us. Her hair is very black and her skin is a different color depending on what time of year it is, and she is always trying to make friends with girls from the outside. But they will never be friends with her because they have friends already, and anyway we're never in the same place for more than a day or two. I don't like it when Violet is sad, but I do like it when Violet plays cards with me because there's no one else to play cards with.

The new girl might be Violet's friend. Violet would like that. But she probably won't stay very long either. There are two kinds of people here: the kind that have always been here, and the kind that only stay a little while. I'm only eleven, which is to say I haven't been remembering things for very long, but I can remember lots and lots of different faces that were here one day and gone the next. I usually don't try to learn any of their names. I know the new girl's name but I won't use it, because if I do then I'll remember it and I have better things to think about. Like learning to ride an elephant. I want to ride an elephant everywhere I go and then people will have to look up to see me and they will be impressed and want to know who I am. And if they laugh at me I can get my elephant to stomp them.

Maybe I'll stomp that new girl, too, so Violet will come back and play cards.

Red Lipstick

There were differences among the small towns they toured, even though they all looked precisely the same. Most of these differences were irrelevant to the Wonder Show. They didn't care how many residents had telephones, whether the movie theater had new features or was still showing *Gone with the Wind,* or if the specials ever changed at the diner. Their stops were short. They didn't stay long enough to get involved. As long as the townsfolk showed up at the ticket wagon with money in hand, one place was no better or worse than another.

Portia had a different view, at first. She looked more closely at each face, because she was searching, and she *made* herself look. But even she began to lose focus after the second week. It was exhausting, training her eyes on so many individual noses and hats and sets of hands, making note of what she saw even as the doubting part of her grew deeper, louder, stronger.

Somewhere between the bottom edge of Ohio and the open span of Kentucky, they crossed the border into Jesusland. That's what Jimmy called it, the part of the country where everyone believed in One Holy Savior and they were quick to crush anyone who carried the seeds of doubt in his heart.

The towns' faces seemed the same. Pawnshops, five-and-dimes, train tracks, churches, new-built houses, factories, more churches, feed stores. But behind the window-eyed storefronts, there was desperation, prayer, regret, blind faith, righteousness, secrets, fear.

Taking a freak show through Jesusland was like dropping a dog into a pack of wolves. It would either be torn apart or slip through unnoticed. Mosco depended on the advance man to tell him whether a town was safe or not — he didn't have the choice of whether to stop or move on (the route card was set and the circus called the shots), but when the advance man painted a red circle in the bottom left-hand corner of the bills he posted outside of town, Mosco told the twins, "Just dancing tonight. No blowoff." And he wouldn't let anyone but Gideon or Violet go into town for supplies.

First stop in Alabama, they were greeted by the red circle, and Mosco sent Gideon and Violet to the grocery store. He grudgingly gave Portia the nod to tag along.

"You've got one hour," he said. "Don't dawdle."

Portia restrained herself from telling Mosco he sounded like her Aunt Sophia. She'd already blamed her various culinary disasters on Sophia's poor teaching — Mosco surely wouldn't appreciate the comparison.

She climbed into the red pickup, and Violet hopped in after her. The truck was narrow, and Portia struggled to keep a precious inch of space on either side of her. The heat was intolerable. She couldn't stand to feel the silk of Violet's going-to-town dress on her thigh, or the stiff brush of Gideon's canvas work pants on her other side. She tugged her skirt down underneath her, but it wouldn't cover her knees.

Should've let my hems down before I ran away, she thought. The shorter skirts made it easier to ride her bicycle, but she needed to find ways to look older if she was going to survive on her own. She'd been trying to talk Gideon into teaching her how to drive, completely without success. But Violet had promised to help her pick out a lipstick at the five-and-dime while Gideon put gas in the truck and did the shopping, so at least she'd have something to work with. She had already informed Jackal that she'd be employing a new hairstyle—the braids weren't fooling anyone, and she hated the way they bounced against her shoulder blades when she walked.

When Violet asked Gideon to drop them off, he said, "Don't you have enough of that junk already?"

"It's for Portia," Violet snapped.

Gideon frowned. His obvious disapproval made Portia itch. *He thinks Violet's a bad influence,* she thought. *But he's the one who introduced us in the first place.*

She cleared her throat, as if to dislodge the words she wasn't saying.

Gideon shook his head. "Fine, whatever. But if you're not back here by the time I'm done cleaning the windshield, I'm leaving without you."

Portia looked back at him over her shoulder as Violet dragged her away.

"He's bluffing," Violet said. "He's always threatening to leave me places, but he never does. Even when I want him to."

"What do you mean?"

"Oh, nothing. Just . . . nothing. Come on."

Woolworth's was across the street from the gas station. Portia could see Gideon through the front window, leaning across the truck, scrubbing at the bugs on the windshield with a wet sponge. His right foot lifted off the ground, his arms extended. He looked like a dancer.

"How about this one?" Violet was at her shoulder with a tube of lipstick, turning it up so Portia could see. It was a deep red, the color of overripe strawberries. "This would look great with your hair."

"Okay," Portia said. She didn't know enough to choose for herself. She could entrust this small choice to Violet, spare herself the mistake, if it was one. "How much?"

Violet shook her head. "My treat, darling. Bad luck for a girl to pay for her first lipstick. It's like the tarot cards. You can't buy them for yourself. You can't pay for something powerful. It has to be given to you." She waved the lipstick like a magic wand. "And this," she said, "is powerful stuff."

Before Portia could ask where Violet got the money to pay for such items, the bell on the Woolworth's door sent its little birdsong through the sticky air. She looked up, expecting to see Gideon, embarrassed to be caught among the strange luxuries of the cosmetics counter.

But it was three boys who entered the store — tall, clean cut, with the shiny scrubbed faces of young men sent into town by their mothers. They looked like a Norman Rockwell composition, the three of them stacked up by the door, until they moved through the doorway and one of them spotted the girls.

"Well," he said, grinning. "What have we here?"

Portia recognized his tone, all false innocence and play. Brewster Falls had its share of boys who liked to follow the road out of town and surprise a wayward girl or two working in the orchard. Fortunately they had all been too scared of old

Bluebeard to try to steal any of his wives. So no real harm was ever done, but the boys sometimes got just brave enough to hide in one of the apple trees and spook the girls. Mister had finally installed a few empty shotguns among the outbuildings and granted the older girls permission to brandish them when necessary.

It was unlikely, Portia thought, that she could use that tactic in the middle of Woolworth's. And if Violet had any of the same itchy feeling Portia had in her legs, it didn't show.

"Gentlemen," she replied genially. "Isn't it a lovely day?"

The boys sauntered toward them. Portia glanced out the window, but Gideon's truck was gone. She looked around the Woolworth's. The only other inhabitant was the old man behind the cash register—his eyes were fixed on the fan limping in lazy circles on the ceiling.

"Sure is," the same boy said. "Y'all must be new in town. I'd remember seeing *you* before."

Violet smiled and appeared utterly charmed. "We're just visiting family for a few days," she purred. "We're cousins. Our grandparents own the feed store down Main Street."

The boy looked perplexed. "Mr. and Mrs. Mason?"

"Yes, that's right," said Violet.

One of the other boys finally found his tongue. "You sure you ain't part of the traveling show?" He sounded angry. Portia could feel her dress sticking to the sweaty small of her back.

Violet giggled. "Of course not! Do we look like *freaks?*" She bit into the last word like a bad-tasting pill.

All three boys just stared, but their foreheads were furrowed with the effort of trying to reconcile what Violet was saying with the improbability of it being true. But before they could get there, Violet grabbed Portia's hand and bolted for the door.

Gideon's truck sat there like a chariot from heaven.

"Everything all right?" he asked as the girls tumbled into the seat.

Violet wriggled her fingers at the pile of confused farmboys peering at them through the Woolworth's picture window. "Just fine," she said.

"How did you know what to say?" Portia asked, once they were on the road and she could breathe again. Gideon drove in his usual silence.

"What do you mean?" Violet gazed out the window at the yellowed land.

"How did you know about the feed store? And Main Street?"

"Oh, that." Violet patted Portia's hand without turning her head. "There's always a feed store, and there's always a Main Street. And," she added bitterly, "there are always rubes like that trying to sniff us out."

Then she reached into her bag. "I didn't forget about you," she said, and handed Portia the gleaming silver tube of lipstick.

It was cold in Portia's palm. Like a shotgun shell.

Violet helped Portia copy a hairstyle from one of the movie magazines, an elaborate twist-and-pin updo that made Portia look at least twenty (or so Violet opined), and showed her how to dab and blot the lipstick until it was perfectly even. It made Portia unpleasantly self-conscious of her mouth, and she wondered if it would be difficult to do her bally, if she was thinking too much about what she looked like. But Violet was delighted and practically pushed Portia out of the trailer in her eagerness to show off her handiwork.

Of course, the first one they saw was Gideon.

He was sitting in the back of the red truck, reading, just as he had been when Portia arrived. Then, he had not seemed the least bit surprised to see her. Now, he sat up and gawped like a fish suddenly deprived of water.

"Doesn't she look terrific?" Violet squealed.

Gideon said nothing. Portia's stomach began to clench, and she fought the urge to run back to the trailer.

"Geez," said Violet. "You are such a *killjoy*, Gideon. Tell her she looks nice!"

Instead, he said, "Can I talk to you?"

Portia nodded.

"Fine," Violet snapped. "I'm going to help Mrs. Collington get ready for the show."

As she marched away, Portia and Gideon stood in silence. Finally Portia said, "I don't have much time. Jackal's waiting for me—"

"What are you doing here?" Gideon asked.

"You know what I'm doing," she said. "I'm looking for Max."

"No, you're not. Not really," he told her. "I've offered to help you, and you've ignored me. You just keep staring at people and writing things down in your notebook. That isn't—"

"What?"

"That isn't how you *find* someone."

He was saying everything she had worked so hard not to tell herself. Looking for Max like this, night after night—it wasn't even like looking for a needle in a haystack. It was like looking for a particular piece of hay.

"I know," she told Gideon. "But I've been in one place all this time. I was living in that house, and I was waiting, and my father didn't come to get me. What if—" She swallowed, took a breath. "What if he knew where I was all along?"

Gideon leaned against his truck and rubbed at the back of his neck. Portia knew now that this was what he did when he was thinking, weighing his words. She found it oddly reassuring.

"You don't want to find him," he said finally. "You want him to find you."

"I want him to be looking," she said.

He nodded.

"I have to keep going," she said.

He nodded again. He did not offer comfort or promises, knowing how hollow they would sound striking against Portia's words. He did not remind her that there were only nine more towns on the route card, ten days before the circus broke down for the last time and lurched east, and the Wonder Show disbanded for another season.

She did not have much time left to shelter with them.

But for now, the bally was waiting.

Kites at Midnight

Most nights Portia rode in the red truck with Gideon driving, her bicycle tucked securely in the bed. She gladly surrendered the trailer to Violet before they left the lot. It was too hot for the two of them, even at night, even with the windows open, and Portia preferred to ride up front. Gideon didn't expect her to talk too much, didn't try to start conversations just to fill the air with words. He let her sit in silence, when she wanted to. She could watch the land moving past and think about the growing distance between her and Mister. She tried not to picture his face too clearly, but kept him indistinct, imagined him getting smaller and smaller as she pulled away.

The caravan drove, their many headlights cutting a narrow path across the prairie. Sometimes they drove all night, sometimes just a few miles. Occasionally, the road would curve, and as the trucks ahead of them followed its arc, their lights illuminated something: the shape of an animal trotting into a field, a dead tree, a collapsing house. They seemed to be parts of some hidden world that emerged only at night and revealed itself quietly, grudgingly. Portia felt privileged and strange to have witnessed these things.

The night after Violet gave her the stolen lipstick, Portia saw a door, standing upright in its frame with no house behind it. It struck her as unbearably sad. But when she pointed it out to Gideon, he laughed.

"The house must have come down in a twister and left the door behind."

"Don't you think it's lonely, though?"

He rubbed at his ear. "Could be. Or maybe the door let the house go. Think how strong it's got to be, standing there by itself. Hasn't been blown over, hasn't been stolen. Hell," he said, "it's probably still locked."

Portia smiled then and allowed herself to fall into a half-sleep, floating between night and day.

She woke with a lurch as the caravan stopped suddenly.

The caravan didn't stop unless they hit a bad patch of road or got lost. Even with the advance man going out a day ahead and putting up red arrow signs to show them the way, wrong turns sometimes got taken, and it made for a foul mood all around. Especially all around Mosco.

"What's going on?"

"Dunno," Gideon said, and put the truck in park, and stepped out into darkness so black that he immediately disappeared. But the headlights were still on, and so Portia could see Jim carrying Jimmy toward her. She rolled down the window. There was just an edge of cold in the air.

"What is it?" she asked Jim.

"Wind's up," he told her. "Full moon, dry ground. Good night for flying."

Portia thought perhaps *flying* was another one of those carny expressions she hadn't learned yet. She had been writing them down in her notebook, phrases like *hey, rube* and words like *donniker,* even though she knew she'd never say them while she was here, because she was still an outsider—and she'd never say them if she went back into the main part of the world, because no one would understand.

A few of the trucks in the line had turned sideways so their headlights were shining at the empty field next to her, and she saw Jimmy and Jim and the Lucasies and Polly and Pippa all marching out to the edge of the field. They were dark shapes carrying dark shapes until more headlights were turned on, and they became people again. And they were carrying kites.

"Where did those come from?" Gideon had come back and was standing next to Portia's window.

"Mosco made them!" Joseph called back. "Out of the old circus posters!"

Jim loped across the field with two kites in hand, one for the twins and one for Jimmy. They stood and doled out twine as he went, Jimmy shouting, "Get way out there!" After a few minutes, Jim stopped and held the kites up over his head. His faded voice came from the darkness: "Ready!"

Polly and Pippa leaned back and started reeling in their twine like they were fishing in the air. Their kite rose slowly, higher, higher, until it was hovering and bobbing above the trees. Then Jimmy's, too, caught the wind and climbed the sky. Gideon walked over to watch.

Mosco appeared, carrying Marie in a picnic chair, which he set down off to the side a bit so no one would crash into her.

He threaded her twine between her toes and patted her knee awkwardly, and then he trotted out into the field to join Jim, thrusting Marie's kite into the air as if he could stick it to the sky if he only threw it hard enough.

Mr. and Mrs. Lucasie stood silently, glowing in the headlights while Joseph galloped around them, laughing his bird-laugh and holding a smaller kite above his head as if it might at any moment lift him off the ground.

Jim's faraway voice shouted, "They're up!"

The truck motors went off one by one, and the headlights too, so the field was dark again, and the kites flew at the moon like dangerous birds. Birds wearing the faces of the circus performers, the ones who would not speak to the freaks, or eat with them, or admit to breathing the same air.

Doula wandered by Gideon's truck. Portia opened the door and followed her.

"Acting like children," Doula muttered.

"I think it's beautiful," said Portia. She heard a little slurping sound. "Doula."

"Porrrtia." *Slurp.*

"Where's Violet?"

Doula grunted. "How should I know? I am not her mother."

Portia muttered, "Lucky for her," and walked the few steps to the trailer door. There was no answer when she knocked. She opened the door. "Violet?"

Violet's bed was empty.

Portia ducked inside and looked around. There were not many places to hide in a fifteen-foot trailer, but she looked in the closet and, finding it empty, scanned what little space there was left, as if Violet might suddenly appear from behind something. There was only the usual clutter of magazines and scarves and discarded clothing.

Then Portia saw something new. A piece of paper, tucked halfway under Violet's pillow.

She stepped over, picked it up, and read, "Dear Mother and Father and Joseph." She stopped. This was not meant for her.

Paper in hand, Portia ran to find Gideon.

"Did you see Violet get in the trailer before we left?"

"No. I guess not. Why?"

"She's gone."

ANOTHER LAST LETTER

Dear Mother and Father and Joseph,

I am sorry I did not come to say goodbye. I knew that you would try to stop me from leaving, and I did not want that to happen. It is better for everyone this way.

I am going to become a very rich and famous actress, and then I will buy a big house for you so you will not have to work ever again.

Do not be sad. Do not worry about me. I will find you when I have made my fortune.

Violet

Silence Is Not Empty

Violet's note did not, of course, comfort her family. It did not keep her mother from crying or her father from clenching his fist around the paper as if he could squeeze more from it than what Violet had written.

He turned to Portia. "Violet said nothing to you? About leaving?"

Portia hesitated. "She talked about it sometimes. But she made it sound like something she would do *someday*. Not something she would do *now*." She looked at Joseph. "I didn't think she meant it. I'm sorry."

"Oh, no," Mrs. Lucasie said. She blew her nose into a yellowed lace handkerchief that she had extracted from some secret part of her dress. "It isn't your fault, darling."

Joseph was silent as a stone.

"Are you all right?" Portia asked.

He did not answer, only walked away with his kite dragging behind him.

"He will be fine," Mr. Lucasie said. "He needs to be alone when he is upset."

Mrs. Lucasie blew her nose again. "I just can't believe no one saw her leave. How did she get away? Maybe we should go back and look for her. She can't have gone very far. Rudolph? Please?"

Violet's father had crushed her note into a tiny globe. He coaxed it open again and smoothed it out against the side of the trailer. Then he folded it gently and put it in his pocket. "We must respect her wishes," he said. "We must believe what she says."

"But she's just a child!" Mrs. Lucasie wailed. "What if something happens to her? We must go and look for her!"

"Antoinette," her husband said, quietly, "you know that we cannot turn back or change direction. We follow the route card, always. Violet knows where to find us. She will return when she is ready."

Mrs. Lucasie sobbed again and leaned against him. He held her, eyes closed, and did not move. The moonlight shone on his white hair.

Somewhere in Portia's mind, a small voice began to whisper. *Tell them people don't come back,* it said. *Tell them what you know. People leave and they don't come back even if you wait like they told you to.*

But she knew that would not help.

The truth often doesn't.

Mosco cleared his throat. "We'd better get a move on. Got to make Rushville by morning."

Slowly, everyone trickled back to the trucks and started them up, and the night filled again with the sound of humming motors and low voices and the yellow glow of headlights.

They drove through the night, inching ever closer to the state line. Town by town, Portia was gaining her freedom. She could hardly begrudge Violet hers.

Portia thought suddenly of Delilah — still stuck, more likely than not, in the only place Portia had ever abandoned. There was always someone going and someone left behind. Portia had been both. She had enjoyed neither. But she knew that leaving a place was sometimes necessary, when you couldn't breathe there anymore, when you weren't yourself because of it.

Maybe that was what had happened to Max, she thought.

But just because everyone else gave up so easily didn't mean she had to do the same. She had already allowed her mother to fade into unreachable memory, let Sophia drop her off at Mister's like a parcel of potatoes, watched Caroline thrash and heave through her last living moments. If there was only one person Portia could retrieve, only one story for which she could write the ending, it was Max.

She would do whatever she had to. There was no other way.

WHAT WAS LEFT BEHIND

They arrived at the edge of Rushville just after dawn. The roustabouts weren't far into their routine — they wouldn't be done for a few hours more and the performers were nowhere to be found, so Mosco sent Mrs. Collington and Mrs. Murphy to the pie car to start breakfast.

"We'll eat early. Get everybody fed and out of the way," he told them.

"Circus eats first," Gideon reminded him.

"They won't make a stink as long as they don't have to see us," Mosco snapped. Then he called after the ladies, "Don't use the good coffee or the potatoes off the top of the bin!"

"Bad coffee, old potatoes," Mrs. Murphy shouted back. "You sure do know how to treat a lady!"

Mosco waved her off and continued hollering at the next person he saw, which happened to be Portia. "Don't you have something that needs doing besides standing around?"

She wasn't at all sure what she was supposed to be doing, since Mosco had decided to spare her from the kitchen — perhaps he felt bad for her, in light of Violet's sudden departure. "I guess," she said.

"Then do it."

"Right."

She was rescued by Gideon, who said she could help him lay out the stage boards and the banners for the bally line.

"I'll just get my tools," he said. "Meet me on the midway."

"How do I know where the midway is? The lot isn't set up yet."

"Midway's always in the same place. Forty paces east of the Big Top."

"Which way's east?"

But he was already walking away.

At least she knew how to find the Big Top. Couldn't miss it, in fact, not with its peak being the highest point on the lot. *I'll just start at the entrance and walk forty paces from there,* she thought. *Only so many directions to go.*

As she passed the Wonder Show caravan line, she noticed a small crowd outside her trailer. Marie, Anna, Doula, Mrs. Murphy, Mrs. Collington, and Polly and Pippa were gathered around in a tight circle, and it wasn't until Portia got right up close that she could see what they were doing.

They were going through Violet's things.

All the items she had left behind were spread out on a blanket on the ground, and the women were bickering over them. Scarves, clothes, hairpins, magazines, a World's Fair souvenir pillbox, a pillow shaped like Texas. Laid out like prizes.

"Stop it!" Portia pushed past Polly and Pippa. "What are you doing?"

Doula held up a worn blue skirt. "Is the code," she said. "Someone leave things behind, we take things they leave."

"What if she comes back?"

Pippa snorted. "She's not coming back."

Portia had told herself the same thing, but for some reason, hearing it said out loud infuriated her. She pushed the twins away from the trailer. "Get out of here!"

Pippa stepped up to shove Portia back, but Polly had planted her feet and wouldn't budge, so Pippa had to settle for swatting at Portia's arm. "You have a lot of nerve, ordering me around! Who do you think you are? You're not even in the *show!*"

Then Portia uttered the forbidden word: "Freak."

And Pippa came back with a worse one: "Normal."

Anna flinched.

Anywhere else in the world, it wouldn't have been an insult. But here, within sight of the midway and the bally, normal was the worst thing to be. It was the strange ones who survived, who turned a profit and got their pictures taken and stayed locked in the memories of everyone who saw them. The twins were royalty here, and they knew it.

And so did everyone else. Which was why none of the others intervened when Pippa finally uprooted Polly enough to lunge at Portia, claws out and ready to strike. Portia ducked out of the way—it was easier to evade the pair than to hold her ground. They were twice her size, after all, even if Polly wasn't a willing participant in the fight. Pippa continued her attack and Portia continued to bob and weave out of reach, until Gideon arrived to find out what was taking her so long to walk forty paces.

"What the hell?" He dropped his tool belt and got hold of the twins around their waist.

"Let me go!" Pippa shouted.

"Me, too!" Polly squeaked. Her face was flushed pink.

"Not until you tell me what's going on here," Gideon said,

and he tightened his grip while the rest of the women took another step back from the scuffle.

Jackal appeared as if out of the air. "I thought I heard the telltale shrieks of a catfight," he said. "Looks like I'm just in time."

Pippa thrust an accusing finger at Portia. "It's her fault! We were just standing here, and she came up and started pushing us around."

"They were stealing!"

Gideon let go of the twins and said to Jackal, "Keep your eye on them," and then he turned to Marie. "Well?"

She shrugged. "We were not stealing. Violet is gone. We were going through what was left behind. You know the code."

Portia was indignant. "How can you just take her things?"

Doula shook her head. "They are not her things. She get them from others who leave, she leave them behind. This is our way." She took Portia by the arm. "Come, I show you."

"But I was going to help Gideon—"

"Go," he said. "It's fine."

"What about what she said?" Pippa huffed. "She accused us of *stealing*. She called us a *freak*."

"Oh, pipe down," Mrs. Murphy told her. "You've done your share of name-calling."

"More than your share, I'd say," Mrs. Collington offered.

They were still arguing as Doula dragged Portia away.

"Wait for me!" Jackal jogged up behind them.

"What you want?" Doula barked.

"Why, only the pleasure of your company, my dear. A leisurely morning. A story or two. And perhaps"—he winked—"a spot to drink."

"You roll cigarettes?"

"Until my fingers go numb, just for you."

Doula rolled her eyes. "You don't listen to anything this one tell you," she said to Portia. "He have head full of money and heart full of lies. Is worst combination."

I can think of worse, Portia said to herself. But she only nodded and let Doula lead her away.

What (Else) Was Left Behind

Doula's trailer looked the same every time Portia was in it—cluttered with junk, nearly choked with it, and yet there were always small rearrangements taking place so nothing was where she thought it would be. The chair she had used last time wasn't in the corner anymore. Doula's card-reading table had migrated to the other side of the room, and her record player was nowhere to be seen. Portia half wondered if these possessions moved themselves, out of boredom, or desperation. Perhaps they were enchanted. Perhaps the rug could fly and the walls could speak and the coat rack turned into a handsome gentleman every night.

Stranger things had happened.

Portia had seen them herself, by now.

"Your abode is a true cavern of wonders, Miss Doula," said Jackal.

"Sit," Doula said, pointing toward the card table.

Jackal and Portia did as they were told, and watched as Doula opened drawer after drawer. Finally, she found the one she was looking for. She pulled out a tin box and brought it to Portia. "Open."

Portia lifted the lid. There was a smaller package inside, canvas, tied with twine.

"Keep going," Doula said.

Probably some kind of trick, Portia thought. *She's going to make me unwrap it seven times, and there'll be nothing inside after all.*

But curiosity (and Doula's insistence) made her continue, and when she unrolled the canvas like a sail, she was rewarded by the sight of . . . more junk. A pocketknife, a dragon carved out of soap, and a box of straight pins.

"Ah," she said.

"You don't know what they mean," Doula snapped. "Like always, I must explain." She sighed dramatically, as if all of this hadn't been her idea in the first place. "Jackal, get me a drink. I tell her the stories."

"I'll get your drink," said Jackal, "but I tell the stories around here. You just sit tight and don't interrupt."

1. THE POCKETKNIFE

His name was Freeman Barnes.

He was billed as The Human Torso, the man without legs or arms, without even a trace of them. He did everything with his mouth: rolled cigarettes, signed his name, everything. He was a religious man and held church services every Sunday from his trailer. He'd get someone to open the window and get himself propped up against the sill inside, and let loose with the Word of God. Played all the hymns himself, on the harmonica.

There were certain things, of course, that he couldn't do for himself. He could get around just fine—moved himself along like an inchworm—but eating was difficult, and dressing himself was next to impossible. Luckily, Freeman managed to get married as easily as most people tie their shoes. Nearly as often, too. He wasn't short on charm, he could sing like an angel, and he made a more-than-decent living on the show. Freeman had plenty to offer his Mrs. Barneses, and he liked being the man of the house. Charity had its place, he believed, and that place was not in *his* trailer. Women never stuck around for long, but there was always a new one waiting in the wings.

Freeman's teeth and lips were strong, and he wanted to make sure they stayed that way or he'd be out of work. So he found himself a pocketknife and took up whittling. Just before he and the sixth Mrs. Barnes took off to start their own show, he carved a set of chess pieces as a wedding present for Ernst and Lily, and a herd of soap dragons for them to give out to the guests.

He was a great believer in marriage, after all.

2. THE SOAP DRAGON

Some folks said it was a marriage made in heaven, but Ernst and Lily always called it "made on earth" instead. They weren't born looking like a matched set. They made themselves into what they became, and it was a long piece of work. They were artists. They had vision.

They called themselves Adam and Eve. Their act was mostly a series of poses that showed off how their tattoos played off each other—he put his arm around her waist, and there was the serpent wound around the Tree of Knowledge on her back.

They stood back to back, and there was the most perfect fleur-de-lis you ever saw, from their shoulders down to their wrists. It was a dance, it was an art gallery come to life.

When they decided to get married, they wanted to celebrate with something really spectacular, but Ernst had always favored elaborate, showy tattoos, and Lily's father had started inking her when she was thirteen. Neither one of them had enough clean skin left for anything big, at least not where they could show anybody else. When they were on stage, Ernst wore a little pair of shorts and Lily had the same, plus a top. They were totally exposed. Almost.

So the rumor was, they got their wedding tattoos where the proverbial sun doesn't shine. A pair of dragons that met up when they—

"Jackal," Doula interrupted. "Is not important. Move along."

"Sorry."

Their wedding was the event of the season. They put a proper ad in *Billboard* so the whole circuit got notice of the date—carnies and freaks came from miles around to celebrate. And everyone was given a soap dragon, hand-carved (so to speak) by The Human Torso, who, in addition, performed the ceremony and serenaded the bride and groom with a lovely rendition of "Hava Nagila" on the harmonica.

Turns out Ernst and Lily were Jewish.

Who knew?

3. THE PINS

Arthur Plumhoff felt no pain. There were all kinds of stories by way of explanation. He'd been in the war, and the shock of what he saw made him numb all over; he was some kind of a warlock; he had elephant skin that only *looked* human. Sometimes they said he'd just been born that way.

Whatever the reason, Arthur could stick himself full of pins until he looked as if he were made of metal. Whole body — face, arms, legs, everything. He even shaved his head and put them all over his scalp, later on. He was billed as The Human Pincushion on account of the act, but by the time I knew him, he was doing more than just pin-sticking. He'd take sewing needles and embroider designs on himself with thread, like Ernst and Lily's tattoos, only Arthur would unravel 'em every night so he could start over the next day.

Afraid of commitment, I guess.

Then he got into audience participation. He'd get ladies to come up on stage and embroider him themselves. They were always squeamish at first, but Arthur would talk them through it and keep promising they weren't hurting him, and pretty soon he'd be covered with hearts and flowers and "Betsy loves Walter" and such. Somewhere along the line Arthur got himself a set of metal rings with needle joints, like earrings, and had Lily put them all around his back. He'd pick a girl out of the audience, hand her a pair of ribbons, and let her thread the rings like shoelaces. Looked like he was wearing a corset from the back. Always got a laugh.

Of course there were always a few hecklers in the crowd,

nonbelievers, doubting Thomases. Arthur may have been numb, but he was prideful, too. Couldn't pass up a challenge. He was a damned fool for a challenge.

We were playing our last show somewhere in Michigan — Houghton Lake, maybe — and some fella dared Arthur to put a sword through his front. We begged him not to, but he said he'd just weave it through under the skin, just like with the pins and needles. I suppose we wanted to see what would happen. Arthur'd never done anything so grand before. It would have changed his show forever.

If it'd worked.

It *looked* as if it worked. He got the blade clear through, in one side and out the other, and the crowd went wild, cheering and calling out like they'd just seen the Second Coming. Arthur up there on stage, strutting around like the king of the barnyard. He kept that thing in him as long as the cheering went on. Then the sound dipped a little, and everyone knows that's when you're done, when the tip turns back against you. Arthur decides to finish with a flourish, so he whips the sword back out, and before you can blink, there's blood everywhere. Fountains of it. Sprayed the whole front row like a garden hose.

Doc said Arthur must have gone too deep, maybe nicked an organ somewhere along the way. Took hours for him to die.

But I tell you true: people are still talking about that show. Arthur Plumhoff, the man who felt no pain.

Jackal poured himself another drink and leaned back in his chair, regarding Portia with a satisfied grin. "There you have it," he said. "A little bit of history. Your very own piece of the past."

She looked at the things on the table—they didn't have names, they weren't even really unique. They could have come from anywhere. "Is it true?" she asked Doula. "Or is it just a story?"

"Only truth is what you can touch. Someone leaves and they are gone for a while, I might think I dreamed them. You might think so, too." Doula tapped the lid of the tin box with a craggy finger. "That is why I keep things. To believe."

She reached into her shawl and pulled out one of Violet's lipsticks.

"To remember," said Doula. She laid the lipstick next to the dragon, the straight pins, and the knife. She rolled them into the canvas, tied the twine, and dropped the bundle back into the box. The snap of the lid sounded like a gunshot.

Jackal fished another glass out of the cupboard behind him, poured an inch of vodka into it, and pushed it across the table to Portia. Then he raised his drink and said, "To Violet."

Forever after, Portia would think of her friend when she heard the ring of glass meeting glass, or felt the burn of vodka in her throat.

The Size of an Empty Space

That night Portia wandered the lot. The circus talent and the roustabouts knew her by now, recognized her from the pie car, so she was not able to blend in as well as she once had. But amid the crowds of strangers, she felt cushioned, protected. These unsuspecting souls would never guess who she was or where she had come from. They were not looking at her, any of them. She was utterly anonymous.

As the lot purged itself of customers after the late show, Portia drew closer to the midway and the waiting colony of trucks and trailers. Most of the performers were already tucked into their dens, but a few were sitting outside, chatting across the narrow gaps between the metal bodies of their homes. They had booked an extra day here — Portia could not remember the name of the town — so there was none of the hushed buzzing of activity that preceded a move. The night was calm, and the air had cooled kindly.

Anna was sitting on the steps of the trailer she shared with Marie, the glossy painted image of her sister watching over her. She smiled when she saw Portia approaching. "Are you all right?" she asked. Her voice was so soft, it was almost lost as soon as it left her body.

"Fine, thank you," Portia replied. She thought of Anna's face, twisting at Pippa's use of that forbidden word. "I'm sorry about that. About before."

Anna's smile wavered a bit but did not fade. "There is a lot that's hard to understand here. A lot of rules. All of us had to learn them, and all of us made mistakes."

It was the most Portia had heard Anna say since she'd arrived. Even more astonishingly, she went on.

"I'm sorry about Violet. You were friends."

"I thought so," Portia said, more bitterly than she meant to.

Anna bobbed her head. "She knew you'd be upset. She knew her family would be devastated. But she made herself leave anyway. She was afraid, if she didn't, that she'd have to stay forever."

"Did she tell you that? Did she talk to you before she left?"

"No." Anna stood, running her hands up and down her arms. The night was cooling rapidly now. "I just know how she feels."

Then she nodded once, stepped into her trailer, and closed the door.

Portia's own trailer was empty. She had her own place to sleep, for the first time in years, and it felt like the biggest empty space in the world. Bigger than the Grand Canyon. Bigger than the craters on the moon. Bigger than the ocean's bed without the ocean in it.

She avoided going to sleep as long as she could. Her nightly ritual of remembering Max and the family stories had lost its power and did not comfort her anymore. Instead, she invented tasks to keep herself awake. She explored every corner of the trailer (which took about fifteen minutes). She put on her lipstick and made movie star faces in the mirror until she got embarrassed and wiped it off. She imagined she was on a train to California. She turned the train around and headed for New York. She made it into a boat and departed for Italy.

She stood in the hallway and put her hands out to touch the sides, to remind herself that this was, in fact, quite a small space and not empty at all.

But when she finally lay down, alone, the trailer walls seemed to breathe and swell outward, away from her, threatening to split themselves apart and drop her into the earth where she was sure a cavernous hole had formed so that she would fall into it and keep falling and fall straight down to hell, where Mister was waiting to roast her like a pig on a spit.

Portia launched herself out of bed and down the hallway to the trailer door, which she flung open and jumped through as if the flames were already licking at her nightgown. Which she imagined they were. Which made her start to run.

She didn't look at the ground, didn't see what tripped her. So she screamed, and she kept screaming until a rough, warm hand wrapped itself over her mouth.

"Shh," Gideon said. "Shh. It's just me."

She felt her heart kicking in her chest, heard her own rapid breath. She let Gideon hold her still until her body began to calm. Neither one of them moved for what seemed like a long time. Finally, Portia broke the spell.

"Mmph."

"What?" Gideon pulled his hand away.

"What are you doing out here?"

"Nothing."

"It's the middle of the night."

His face was barely visible in the darkness. She could only just make out the line of his nose, his chin like a rock breaking the surface of water.

"I thought . . . you might be lonely," said Gideon.

Portia felt around with her bare foot and found the blanket on the ground, still warm from where Gideon had been sleeping.

"Oh," she said.

"So," he said.

They stood silent for an excruciating moment, until Gideon cleared his throat and said, "Good night, then."

"Good night," Portia answered. She stepped backwards and turned to go inside, then paused in the doorway and whispered over her shoulder: "Thank you."

She did not wait for a response. She trusted he had heard.

GIDEON

I know she's in trouble. I've seen people in trouble before. But I don't know if I can help her. I've never been able to save anyone before. I said I'd give up trying to save anyone else. I promised myself.

I know. It's stupid. You can change, but not that much.

I want to erase whatever happened to her.

She keeps telling me she's happy here. I don't think she's lying. But I'm not sure happiness is what matters. It's a luxury, happiness. It's something like a falling leaf or a certain shape in a cloud. It lands. It changes. It can't last.

It's a gift, sure. But it can't last.

Anyway, if she won't tell me what she's going to do, how am I supposed to help her? A man's got trouble, he'll either talk about it or he won't. He'll either tell it to you or keep it to himself. Women, though. They'll tell you a little piece and keep the rest, and no matter how many ways you try to dig the rest of it out, you can't get any more of the story.

Maybe if I'd had sisters I'd understand.

I just wish I knew what was haunting her.

Maybe then I could do something.

JOSEPH

I thought the new girl would leave, but Violet did instead.

Mother has been crying for two days, and Mosco had to change the sign on the stage to say FATHER AND SON instead of FAMILY because if Mother was up there crying, people would think she was being mistreated. Father says Violet will be back but I don't think he believes it. He sounds very empty when he says it, like he is a tire and someone has let all the air out of him. She always talked about leaving and none of us thought she really would because she didn't really have anywhere to go. She doesn't know anyone we don't know. Does she?

Violet is gone and the new girl is still here. Sometimes she tries to talk to me but I don't want to hear her say "I'm sorry" again, so I just ignore her. It doesn't matter if she is sorry. Violet is gone and no one will play cards with me now.

I wish I had my elephant. I would stomp that new girl and then I would find Violet and bring her back. We would ride my elephant together like a prince and a princess and I would never think Violet's black hair was ugly again.

PUNKS

Portia was suspicious when Joseph offered to show her his favorite place, but she knew he'd been lonely without Violet, and she decided that even if he was up to something, she felt sorry for him just enough to go along with it.

"It's this one," he said. He'd led her to a trailer she'd never noticed before, one that looked older than the rest. It was made of wood instead of aluminum, and it was plain, painted a dark red, without any decoration. It sat alone at the edge of the cluster.

"Who lives here?" Portia asked.

"The punks," said Joseph.

"Who are the punks?"

"They're the oldest part of the show," he said. "They were here before Mosco came, and he had to keep them because it's bad luck to leave them behind. Come on."

The door was unlocked.

"They won't mind us just walking in?"

Joseph laughed. "The punks don't mind anything. Come *on*." He skipped up the steps and beckoned impatiently for her to do the same. He was practically hopping up and down, he was so excited. Portia sighed and followed.

"Close the door," Joseph said.

She was getting more suspicious by the second, but she was also getting curious, so she closed the door behind her. She could barely see anything, it was so dark inside. It was as if the whole interior of the trailer had been painted black, as if there were a wall in front of her. It was incredibly hot. She couldn't imagine anyone living in here.

"This is it," she heard Joseph say.

"This is what? I can't see a thing. Can you turn on the lights?"

"No lights," he said. "I'll open the curtains."

There was the sound of him stumbling, and then sunlight flooded the room. The first thing Portia saw was the dust in the air, like a blizzard, and then she saw the jars.

Huge glass jars. Lined up like soldiers. Full of liquid and blobby shapes that didn't look like anything, until she got closer and saw they had arms and legs and faces.

Faces with dead, open eyes.

Portia screamed.

"Do you like them?" Joseph hissed. "I think they like you."

The tone in his voice, the sheer satisfaction, sliced through her horror and held her scream fast. She wanted to close her eyes and feel her way out of the trailer blind, so she wouldn't have to see the rest of the jars and their gruesome contents, but instead she forced her hands to her sides and looked straight at Joseph. He blinked uncomfortably, edged away from a thick ray of sunlight cutting into the room. His hand itched at his pants pocket where his sunglasses were nestled.

Portia had a choice. She could outdo him in cruelty, pretend to enjoy her surroundings, and thank him for bringing her. Or she could act scared, run away, and give him some small measure of power. Even if neither of them believed in it. It was a concession she was willing to make.

But before she could do anything, Joseph threw her aside and lunged for the door. He opened it with one hand while the other struggled at his pocket. Portia heard the sound of fabric tearing as Joseph wrenched the glasses out of their hiding place and slapped them onto his face.

He slammed the door behind him.

"Well," Portia told the punks, "that's that."

She tried to open the door, halfheartedly, and found what she had expected: it was locked. The trailer immediately felt smaller, the glass jars more numerous, the air tighter around her like a tourniquet. She pulled the curtains closed again, bathing herself in darkness, so at least she wouldn't have to look at the punks watching her, bobbing in their individual oceans, waiting to see what she would do next. She sank to the floor and stretched her legs in front of her.

No one knew she was here. No one except for Joseph, and it was clear to her now that he would never be her friend.

She thought of Delilah then, and of Caroline, and of all the girls she had known at Mister's. How many of them would call her a friend? How many had wondered where she was? They each existed so separately, despite sharing the same space and the same fearful hatred of the same man. How many of those girls would come to her rescue at a time like this, when she was trapped in a small, dark place?

But she knew the answer, felt it pricking the back of her skull.

She could not wait for anyone else to save her.

She could only save herself.

What Comes After

They were obvious when they arrived, because they were dressed in dark suits and driving a dark car, and they were not dusty. They were strangers, but not strange. They did not look away from anything. Their eyes were not on the ground. Two men, one taller than the other by a head (just one head, a normal-size head), both of them wearing hats and ties that looked as if they had never been undone.

Marie was the first one they spoke to.

"We're looking for this girl," the taller man said, and held up a photograph. He did not attempt to hand it to her.

It was not unusual for men in suits to come looking for someone at the carnival. Marie had been presented with photos before, but usually they were mug shots of hard-looking men, and if she ever recognized them, it didn't matter because they were roustabouts who had collected a couple of checks and were already long gone, and she could only say, "Yes, he was here. I don't know where he is now."

So Marie did not expect to see Portia's eyes, her face, Portia's hair, under the man's fingers where he pinched the photograph so it wouldn't fly away in the breeze. Even though he had said "this girl," she wasn't prepared. She faltered.

"Yes . . . er, no. I don't think I've seen her. But we go through so many towns . . ."

"She isn't traveling with you?"

"With me? Oh, no."

"She isn't part of your show?"

"Not unless she has flippers or a tail." Marie forced herself to laugh and fluttered her eyelashes at the shorter man, who remained silent.

"Mind if we look around?" the taller man asked.

Marie scanned the midway and saw Gideon hunched next to the bally stage, tapping on the wood as if he were hunting for treasure. Surely the men had seen him too, and if they showed him the picture and his poker face was no better than Marie's, they would know more than enough. Too much by far.

"I'd be happy to show you—" Marie started.

"That won't be necessary," the man said. "We've done this before."

"Well, good luck, then," she said, and turning to go, she tangled her feet and fell to the ground.

Luckily, the men were not without compassion, at least the shorter one, who immediately crouched down to help Marie stand. "Are you all right?" he asked. His voice was surprisingly gentle, even kind.

Marie looked over his shoulder and saw Gideon running toward her. "Oh, yes," she said, more loudly than necessary. "It's difficult to keep my balance sometimes. I'm sure you understand."

"I couldn't possibly," said the man. He tipped his hat and went to stand next to his partner again just as Gideon arrived and said, "What happened?"

"Oh, it was nothing, you know how I take a wrong step sometimes, Gideon, perhaps you could help me to my trailer, lovely to meet you, gentlemen, I hope you find what you're looking for."

"But—"

"Come along!" Marie said. "I haven't got all day!"

Looking utterly perplexed, Gideon did as he was told.

"You've never taken a wrong step in your life," he said. "Did one of those guys knock you down?"

"Where's Portia?"

"I don't know. Why?"

"Because," Marie said over her perfect and swiftly moving shoulder, "they're looking for her. And I don't think they mean well."

JOSEPH

There were two men. One was tall and one was short. I thought maybe they were a new act — they looked like normals, but they could have been rubber-skinned men or contortionists. With marvels, you can't tell until you see what they can do. Freaks, you know as soon as they walk by you.

Marvels get to hide if they want to. Blend in with the normals. I used to think of ways I could do that, too — makeup, maybe, or some kind of costume — but I gave up eventually. Not because I stopped wanting to blend in. It just started to seem, I don't know, like wishing on pennies in a fountain. You make a wish and throw your penny and then you realize that it's just going to sit there under water until someone takes it out. It's a penny. There's no magic to it.

I keep my pennies in my pocket now.

I watched the men for a while, to see if they did anything interesting, but they were just walking around and showing something to people. I couldn't see what so I got closer and then I could see it was a picture, and then I got a little closer and I could see it was a picture of a girl, and when I got close enough

to see it was a picture of *her,* the tall man said, "Holy shit."
Which meant he saw me, too.

The short man had the picture and he held it up and asked
me, "Have you seen this girl?" I didn't know what they wanted
but I don't believe in lying so I said, "Yes."

Except that's a lie. I lie all the time. When Mother asks me if
I've been near the elephants again, I lie. When Mosco accused
me of being the one who switched Marie's knives around, I lied
then, too. (I didn't really mean to switch the knives, though.
I was just looking at them and then I guess I put them back
wrong. It wasn't really my fault—they all look the same.)

I could have lied to the short man, too.

But I wanted her to go away. She made me miss Violet too
much. And maybe if she went away, Violet would come back
and things would go back to the way they were before.

So I told the short man, "Yes, I've seen her."

I guess I'm sorry.

Caught

She was alone when the men found her. Portia had never seen them before, but she recognized them. The dark of their suits was the same dark that came from the windows of Mister's house, the same dark that hung in Mister's eyes. They looked like they'd been made out of shadows.

She was not with anyone.

She was wearing a red dress.

She was reading the list of names in her notebook.

She was thinking of Gideon's face.

She was alone.

She watched the two men coming for her, and she did not move.

But then she heard them. Faraway voices, coming closer, all of them calling her name. And then she saw them: Mosco, Marie, Gideon, and Jackal, running. The two men in suits did not run — they walked steadily and did not look behind them at the approaching pack of voices. They were coming for her, and she could not move.

Everyone got to her at about the same moment.

Portia stood up.

"How did you know where to find me?" she asked Short.

Tall answered, "The little boy told us."

"What little boy?" she asked Short.

"The ghosty one," said Tall.

"I'm gonna kill that kid," Mosco muttered.

"His name is Joseph," Portia told Short.

"I do the talking," Tall told her.

"Too bad," Portia said. "I'm not tall enough to look you in the eye. And if I'm going to go anywhere with anyone, it's going to be someone I can look in the eye."

"Wait a minute," Gideon gasped, still breathing hard from running. "Who says you're going anywhere?"

"The man who hired you," Portia said to Short. "Is he ever going to give up?"

Short shook his head.

"Is he ever going to let me go?"

He shook his head again.

Portia pointed at Short and said to Gideon, "That's why."

"That's . . ." He put his hand to his temple and rubbed at it, as if he could dislodge the word he was looking for.

"Brave?" Portia offered.

"Ridiculous," said Gideon. "You're going to give up because he won't? It doesn't make any sense."

"It's not just that. You were right. This is no way to find someone." She reached for Gideon's hand. She did not care what the others thought anymore. She wanted to imprint her touch on him while she had the chance, to make him understand. "I have to go back to where I started before I can figure out where to go next. I'm just hiding here. I can't hide here forever."

Gideon did not pull away. He did not move. He simply looked at her.

His eyes were flecked with gold.

She would not cry.

She let go of his hand.

"Okay, then," Tall said. "Let's go."

He started toward the black car, reached for Portia's arm as though he was sure she'd try to run. But she knew as well as he did, maybe better, that there was nowhere to go. She sidestepped his hand and walked just behind him, with Short a half-step behind her.

Suddenly Tall stopped. He looked back and scanned the cluster of trailers. Then he looked at Portia.

"Where's the bicycle? He told us to make sure we got the bicycle, too."

She pointed, silently, to Gideon's red truck, where the bicycle lay nestled in its bed. Tall strode over and hauled it out, came back with it hoisted over one shoulder. "Let's go," he said again, and the black car was right there, waiting to swallow her whole.

Meanwhile

There was something else.

Mister still had her file.

All summer Portia had searched the crowds. For Max, for Sophia, for her aunts, her uncles, her cousins, anyone familiar. She thought she would find them. And she wasn't sure if she didn't because they weren't there, or because she couldn't remember well enough what they looked like.

The only thing she was sure of was this:

Mister had a file on each and every girl who resided at The Home. That file contained information. And information was the one thing that Portia couldn't make for herself. She could make a life, a future, a new dress, friends, pies, conversation, noise, peace. She could probably even learn to live with what she'd done to Caroline. But she could not let Mister keep the story of what had happened to her family.

It did not belong to him.

PART THREE

RETURN

The drive was shockingly brief. For all the faces she'd seen, breaths she'd taken, meals she'd eaten, thoughts she'd had, songs she'd heard, all the stories, steps, dollars, dust, mosquitoes, stars—she had not managed to put much distance between herself and Mister. She had imagined herself in an unreachable place, another world, like a child with her hands over her face who thinks herself invisible.

But the names of all the towns she'd been to fit on one small slip of cardboard, which she still had in her pocket.

Short drove, and occasionally looked at Portia in the rearview mirror, but he remained utterly silent. Tall, too. She wondered if they felt guilty.

But they must do this all the time, she thought. *It's their job.* And that made her sadder than anything, to think there were men in the world whose whole purpose was to bring people back to the places they had tried to escape.

She watched the still, dry land roll itself out along the road, and when it blurred through her tears, she wiped her eyes with her sleeve. The wet spots on the fabric looked like ink stains, or fingerprints.

She hoped they dried before she got to Mister's.

But this was not a day for any of Portia's wishes to come true, and the spots were still faintly visible when the black car pulled into the driveway. It was just like the first time she'd been delivered there by Aunt Sophia, and she suddenly felt a strange kind of attachment to the black-suited men, as if they were more family she was about to lose.

"Please," she whispered, "don't leave me here. Please."

Tall sighed and said, "She lasted longer than I thought she would. Usually they start this routine as soon as we find 'em."

Short looked up through the windshield and finally spoke. "Give her a break. I wouldn't want to stay here, either. Place gives me the creeps."

Portia had expected his voice to sound rusty like a dry hinge, but it was soft, gentle. It reminded her of Max's voice, which, to her embarrassment, brought a fresh round of tears.

"Geez," said Tall, "I hate it when they cry."

"You have always lacked compassion," Short remarked.

"Compassion don't pay the bills."

"Well, anyway," said Short, and he turned, extended his hand over the back seat to give her a piece of paper. It was a business card.

KIMBLE BROS.

PRIVATE INVESTIGATORS

READING 4-1136

Portia put it in her pocket with the route card.

"What are you doing?" asked Tall.

"You never know who your next client might be," remarked Short. "You looking for someone?" he asked Portia.

She nodded.

"See?" said Short. "Everybody's lost someone. It's what makes our line of work so rewarding."

They sat in silence for a moment.

"Well," said Tall, "let's get this over with." He opened his door, got out of the car, and reached for Portia's door handle, all of which gave Short just enough time to turn again and say,

"Sorry, kid."

Then Tall was pulling her out of the car, and like a specter, or a bad dream, Mister was on the porch.

"Welcome home," he said.

BLUEBEARD'S CLOSET

Portia tried not to breathe too deeply. The air was hot and stale and swimming with dust—made, she imagined, from tiny pieces of paper and cardboard that had broken away from the boxes of files all around her. She felt as if she were inhaling the stories of all the wayward girls, as if she were actually breathing ghosts.

She could hear sounds from other parts of the house. Footsteps and muffled voices, the occasional creak or bump from the house itself, but nothing that gave her any comfort. Mister had put her in the secret room (no longer a secret to anyone now) without any indication of when she might be let out. Delilah came twice a day with bread and apples and water. From counting her visits, Portia knew it had been three days. Three days that felt longer than the entire time she'd been away.

She wanted to picture Gideon's face but stopped herself, in case she couldn't see him. It already felt, too much, as if she'd never been anywhere but Mister's. She had had reasons for coming back. It *had* made sense at some point. It must have, or she would have fought harder when Short and Tall came after her.

But whatever her thoughts had been, they were now as faint as breath in winter air.

If she could only find the box of matches and the candle, she could put her time to good use and search the files. Mister had taken her notebook along with the rest of her things, but it didn't matter—she had memorized the list of names by now, and she had spent long enough thinking about the graveyard girls. She was here for herself this time. But after exploring every nook and corner, all she'd found was a lot of cobwebs and one dead mouse. Holding the mouse in her hand, Portia felt her childish imagination lurch to life like an old carousel, and she brought herself to tears with a story about how the mouse had died all alone in this dark place. She let a torrent of sadness wash over her, too tired to fight, too tired to pretend she didn't care.

Now she simply sat, her knees pulled up to her chest, and tapped a rhythm on the dusty floor with her boot heels.

She had lulled herself so thoroughly that she didn't hear Delilah approaching, and her stomach skipped when the little door swung open.

"Dinner," Delilah sang. She leaned to set the plate and the glass on one of the boxes just inside the door and started to close it again.

"Wait," Portia whispered. "What day is it?"

Delilah smiled. "What difference does it make?"

Portia couldn't quite say why she wanted to know, except that she still had the Wonder Show's route somewhere in her memory. If she knew the date, she might be able to figure out where they were. To be with them in her head, standing on the bally or watching the road roll by from Gideon's truck.

"I just want to know."

Delilah stepped into the room. She kept one hand on the door frame behind her as she squatted in front of Portia.

"You don't get it, do you?" she said. "He is never going to let you leave again. He might never even let you out of this room, angry as he is. So it does not matter what day it is, or what month, or what year. This is it. This is all there is for you now."

Delilah sounded different, more refined. More like Mister.

"Did he tell you to say that?" Portia asked.

Delilah smiled again. "No. I just happen to know how he thinks. He's been helping me with my reading. He can be very kind, when he wants to be."

Portia's stomach flipped again, unpleasantly. "Why does he care so much that I ran away?"

"It wasn't the running away. Girls have run away before." Then she added, "Although no one has ever taken his bicycle."

"That's what this is about? The bicycle?"

"Of course not," Delilah said. "It's because of Caroline."

No matter how many times she had said it to herself, tried to absolve herself, tried to forget, hearing Caroline's name in the dusty air was like seeing her die all over again.

But how did Mister know that she had given Caroline the poison? How did he know she had been in this room before, found the bottle, and taken it from here? She had been so careful not to tell any of the other girls about the files. The only other one who knew was . . .

"You!"

Delilah stood up. "What?"

"You told him!" Portia's voice caught in her throat. "You told him?"

Portia watched Delilah's face as it struggled to decide what expression it wanted to wear. It settled on something like irritation.

"Yes. I told him."

"But . . . why?"

"You keep asking questions when the answers don't matter. Here's where you are. What do you care about why? Why don't get you anywhere."

But it did matter, to Portia. After all the stories she'd learned from Jackal, all the tales she'd heard from Mrs. Collington and Doula and Violet and everyone else, she had come to believe that knowing where she'd come from was much more important than knowing where she was going next. The future would always be uncertain. Who she was, that came from the past.

"Tell me. Please."

Exasperated, Delilah smacked her hand against the door frame. "Because you promised me. I brought you here, and you promised you'd pay me back, and then you just left." She leaned in, ever so slightly, and lowered her voice. "You left me here. And I saw you go. So, yes. *I told him.*"

Then she took a deep breath, coughed, and folded her hands together. "Now if you'll excuse me, I have work to do."

Portia felt her neck getting hot. It had been a long time since she'd had cause to be so angry at someone. It almost felt good.

"So that's it then, Delilah?" she hissed. "You go back to the kitchen and bring me bread and water and what? You wait for me to die here?"

Delilah shrugged. "You know as well as I do, when Mister gets an idea in his greasy head, there ain't — *isn't* anyone who can change his mind."

"What idea?"

"How should I know? I'm just the kitchen girl."

And she slammed the door behind her.

THE BIG IDEA

Five meals later, Portia was set free.

Except that there was very little freedom involved.

He sent Delilah to fetch her, as if Portia were a disobedient pet. The two girls exchanged no words as the one escorted the other from the not-so-secret room, down the hall, and into his study.

He sat in his wing-backed chair, facing the fireplace. His head crested the top of the chair like a dark sun on the horizon.

He did not speak.

Delilah left her at the door. Portia searched her face for any sign of apology, of regret or sympathy, but the girl held her blank expression. Portia recognized the look. It was the same kind of forced disinterest that everyone wore on the midway as they approached the sideshow, the same determination not to look excited. Not to look like anything. To make a mask of their own faces.

Mister waited until he heard Delilah close the door. Then, rising slowly, he turned and treated Portia to the same repulsive grin he'd worn when she first arrived at The Home. "I'll

skip the pleasantries," he said. "We have so many things to dis-
cuss."

She held her tongue. There was nothing to say. Yet.

Mister strolled across the room and stood next to his desk
chair, waved one spidery hand at the chair on the other side,
and waited for her to sit down before he did the same. It was
oddly familiar — as if all the days when she'd sat in the same
spot, wearing the same dress, feeling the same mix of revulsion
and dread, were now swirling together through time. Erasing
the borders of days and weeks so there was no measure of time,
no past, no future. Only this room. Only this moment, over
and over again.

"Well," said Mister as he leaned back in his chair, "what do
you have to say for yourself?"

She felt afraid and hated herself for it. She pictured herself
on the bally, the day that Jackal had told her his story. *Truth is
not what the audience wants,* he'd said. And she knew he was
right. Mister would never know her as she actually was — he
knew a version of her, a disobedient child in need of punish-
ment. That was whom he spoke to now, and that was who
would answer.

She shrugged and petulantly replied, "What do you want
me to say?"

He raised one eyebrow. "Tell me why you did it."

"I don't know."

Mister studied her for a long moment. "Tell me," he said
again.

His voice was getting harder, colder, and Portia knew she
was pushing him. She also knew he would push back.

She shrugged again and crossed her arms. "No."

Could he see over the desk, see her knees shaking like cornered animals?

"Tell" — he leaned forward now — "me."

She would not let herself look scared. If Delilah could keep her mask on, if all those rubes on the bally could do it, so could Portia.

"I don't owe you an explanation," she said. "I don't owe you anything."

He laughed then, a dry sound like old wood breaking apart. "Oh, but you do," he said, his voice low. "You owe me *every-thing*. Do you want to know why?"

She tilted her head ever so slightly, offering one ear.

"Because I fed you, sheltered you, clothed you, when no one else would. Because I kept you alive. And because I sent those men to get you instead of calling the police."

"Should I thank you now?" Her voice sounded like every spoiled little girl she'd seen on the midway, whining for popcorn and cotton candy and one more ride on the Ferris wheel. It made her feel as if she were channeling someone else. And it made Mister furious.

He stood up, pounded one hand on the desk, and bellowed, "You murdered my wife!"

The air stood still, frozen, waiting. Portia swallowed and forced words from her gripping throat. "It wasn't . . . I didn't mean . . ."

Mister sat down, brushed the lapels of his jacket as if he were smoothing the bristled fur of some wild animal. He detested such displays of emotion. Composed once more, he said,

"Of course you didn't. But still, there must be consequences. Obviously I can't let you leave here again."

There was only one way he'd kept girls here before.

"I will never marry you," Portia spat.

Mister's face twisted as if he'd just tasted something vile. "I should hope not," he said. "Don't flatter yourself, my dear. I have no intention of marrying again. It just never seems to work out for me."

"Then, what?" Her voice nearly broke. "Why would you want me to stay if you hate me so much?"

Mister sighed. "Oh, Portia. You have never understood this place properly." He leaned back once more, wove his long fingers together, and settled them on his chest. "The very essence of the McGreavey Home for Wayward Girls is the *girls*. Without the *girls*, there is no life here. There is no purpose."

This, Portia supposed, was the way he spoke to parents, to the townspeople, to anyone from Outside who would listen. He sounded like a preacher delivering a familiar sermon.

"And the truly beautiful part is the transformation. Girls are brought here for many different reasons, but then they find each other, they merge. They all become the same. They become better." He raised an eyebrow in Portia's direction. "Of course, some need more time than others to complete their metamorphosis. But I am a patient man. I will keep them for *as long as it takes*."

The last five words swept over Portia like a blanket made of ice.

"You see, Portia?" Mister hissed. "It is not that I *want* you to stay. But I cannot let you leave. You are still a work in progress."

He slowly opened a desk drawer, and her notebook appeared

in his hand. He set it down, flipped through the pages until he came to her list of names. He tapped the paper with one long finger. "Like so many others, Portia, you have resisted my efforts. And like them, you must be dealt with."

"Are you going to kill me, then?" she asked. "Like you killed them?" She tried to make her words sound hard, tried to fire them like a bullet. Her only weapon.

Mister started, his hand twitching on the notebook's open face. Then he laughed, the same dead, dry sound as before. "I didn't *kill* anyone. Those girls are every bit as alive as you and I. At least, I think they are. Not many of them have kept in touch, you see."

"What did you do to them?"

He smiled. "I gave them new lives," he crowed. "It's the perfect arrangement, really. There are so many enterprising men out west, farmers and miners and general store owners. And they all need hard-working women at their sides. I simply bring them together. For a small fee, of course."

"But," Portia sputtered, "the graves—"

"Empty, my dear. Just in case the families come looking for their girls." He leaned forward a bit. "Of course, they never do."

Finding out that Mister wasn't actually a serial murderer was quite a bit less comforting that she might have expected. Portia called up what little bravado she had left. "You won't get away with this," she told him. "You can't just send me wherever you want and marry me off."

"But there's no one to stop me," he said. He reached into the drawer again. Pulled out a thin folder. Tossed it at Portia.

The folder caught the edge of the desk and spilled its contents on the floor. She saw her name in Sophia's handwriting, the letter her aunt had written so long ago to ask Mister to take Portia in. She saw other notes in Mister's writing, spiked and gnarled like winter branches.

Saw the blood-red word stamped across the front: DECEASED.

"No," she whispered.

"They're *dead*," he replied, savoring the word. "Your aunt knew your parents could never come back for you. She knew it even before she brought you here. And she didn't live much longer, either. Terribly unlucky, your clan."

"You're lying."

Mister waved his hand at the scattered pages on the floor. "It's all there. Parents: deceased. Aunt: deceased. Rest of the gypsy-wagon clan: whereabouts unknown."

Her throat felt full of hot stones. All this time, all of the faces she had examined, and the notes she'd made, and the searching. She had never had a chance of finding Max. She had come back, given up her only chance of freedom, for nothing.

"There is no one left, you see. You are—"

A flash outside the window.

A face, far above where a face ought to be.

It was Jim.

Mission of Mercy
(and a Bit of Revenge)

It had taken four days for them to find her. And their arrival produced the one and only genuine scream Portia ever heard come out of Mister's mouth.

Within minutes, they were all lined up in the living room, like some otherworldly army battalion, standing at attention. Mrs. Collington and Mrs. Murphy and the Lucasies (even a glowering Joseph), Jim, Jimmy, Mosco, and Marie. Mister was pressed against the wall at the far end of the room, waving a fireplace poker like a sword.

"Stay back!" he bellowed. "Don't come any closer!"

"Oh, honestly," said Mrs. Collington, "I do wish you'd stop that."

"Making a damned fool of himself," muttered Jimmy.

Portia couldn't resist kissing Marie on the cheek, for effect, though she did restrain herself (just barely) from climbing onto the couch to greet Jim the same way. Then she took her place next to Mosco. Looking down, she could see the pearly handle of the knife he'd tucked into his belt.

"What's that for?" she whispered.

"Just in case this doesn't go as planned."

"Where's Gideon? And Jackal?"

"Guarding the trucks. And we thought we'd get a better reaction if we left the normals out of it. No offense."

"None taken."

Mister finally regained a bit of his composure and seemed doubly angry for having lost it on account of anyone connected to Portia. "What is the meaning of this? Who are you . . . people?"

"Never mind who we are," Mrs. Murphy said tartly. "We've come for Portia."

"Go get your things, darling," said Mrs. Collington.

But before she could take a step, Mister found another hefty dose of bravado. "She's not going anywhere." It was that low and steely voice he used, the one that made Portia's hairs stand on end. She froze.

"We expected you might object," Mosco said. "That's why we came prepared to buy out her contract."

"Contract?" Mister spat. "There's no contract. She *belongs* to me."

"But you are a businessman, no?" asked Marie.

Mister glared at her.

"You would be foolish to refuse such a deal," Marie went on. "We will give you a fair price and"—she winked at Portia—"you will be rid of this troublesome girl."

"But you see," said Mister, "I do not want to be rid of her. I missed her terribly while she was gone. The house was so quiet without her. So empty. So *dead*."

Portia felt the ghosts of Caroline's hands in hers.

Smooth-voiced and calm as milk, Mister said, "I am not

finished with her yet. And when *I* decide it's time for her to go, I can get a very good price for her through . . . other channels."

With the poker still in his hand, he took a few steps toward the group. Jimmy growled like a dog, but Mister kept coming. His fear had been scattered by his fury, and this talk of setting Portia free, even for money, was bringing him back to life. "You may leave," he said, "the way you came in."

"You're out of your mind if you think we're leaving her here with you," Mosco informed him.

"Portia" — Mister almost sang her name — "there is more. About your *family*."

Even though she didn't believe him, the word, that one word, brought a wave of longing that nearly knocked her over. But it wasn't the same longing she'd felt all summer, looking for Max on the midway in town after town. It was for something else.

"I *will* tell you. As soon as you send these . . . people away. You know you belong here. You have nowhere else to go." He smiled and took a step toward her. Just her. "We need you here, Portia. You won't be so selfish again, will you? Not after what happened to Caroline?"

Another step.

"She trusted you, Portia. She trusted you, and you betrayed her."

And another.

"You killed her, my dear."

"Nonsense!" shouted Mrs. Collington.

"No," said Portia, "it's true."

And it *was* true. But it didn't matter anymore. Portia felt her mind open, as if she had found a clearing in the woods, and she remembered what she hadn't been able to while she'd been locked in the secret room. Her reasons.

"It's why I came back," she told them. Told herself. "I did want my file, but I think I needed to see this place again, too, to make sure it was real. To make sure it really happened."

"What did, dear?" asked Mrs. Collington.

"All of it," Portia told her. "Everything. My life."

This was what she had wanted: the chance to go back to the place where life had turned to face the wrong direction, the chance to pull it back like a headstrong pony and take it where it should have gone before. She could not bring Caroline back. She could not even save Delilah now. It was too late.

But she would not throw herself away to atone for her sins.

Mister would be the end of her. And she was not ready to end.

She turned to Marie. "Help me," Portia said, and Marie nodded.

"How sweet," Mister sneered. "But you should have stayed where you were."

Portia felt the air around her crackling like radio static, pushing her, pulling her, trying to decide, stay, go, run, scream, something, anything, *move*.

"Time to do your penance," said Mister, and he raised the poker.

She reached behind Mosco, snatched the knife from his belt.

She dropped to Marie's feet, set the handle of the knife in place.

She made a wish.

She watched the knife fly, saw it pierce Mister's forearm,

thrust itself deep into his flesh. He staggered back, dropped the poker, clutched his arm to his stomach.

"Wicked girl," he gasped. "Murderer."

"Maybe I am," Portia said. But his words had no teeth anymore, and he couldn't keep her here.

"You have nowhere to go," Mister hissed.

"Yes, she does," Joseph said quietly.

"She's coming home with us," said Mrs. Murphy.

"Keep the knife," said Mosco. He picked up the papers, stuffed them back into the folder, and tucked it under his arm. He nodded to Marie. "Let's go," he said.

And they ushered Portia out of the house on the hill — the strongman, the armless girl, the bearded woman, the fat lady, the giant, the dwarf, and the wild albinos of Bora Bora.

SOPHIA'S LETTER

Dear Sir,

I am writing to request your assistance with my niece. Portia has been in my care for four years, and though I promised my brother that I would care for her until his return, I have recently learned of his untimely and tragic death. (Though I could have told him that working with circus elephants was ill advised, had he asked my advice, which he never did.) Portia's mother passed away some years ago — the circumstances of her death have never been entirely clear, and Portia herself does not know that both of her parents are now residing with Our Heavenly Father. It is my own burden that I cannot bring myself to tell her. If you should choose to share this information, I will, of course, defer to your expertise in the matter.

Portia has a generous heart and a wild imagination — she comes by these qualities through our ancient bloodline, and someday they will serve her well. I regret to say that I was born without these traits, and I find that I am unable to encourage or even manage the child. A life with other girls, some of whom may become as sisters to Portia, must surely be better. I pray for your kind intervention, dear sir, and I remain your humble servant,

Mrs. Sophia Remini Stoller

GRAVEYARD GIRLS

Gideon was waiting by the trucks with Jackal and Doula and Anna. "Are you all right?" he asked Portia. "Is that blood on you?"

"Not mine," she said wearily.

"Sorry we weren't there to help. I guess we weren't exciting enough to come along for the adventure." He put a hand to her cheek and said, "You're all right?"

She nodded. Then she turned to Mr. Lucasie. "I thought you said you never changed direction, that you always follow the route card. But coming here . . . it was completely out of your way."

He smiled. "Rescuing damsels in distress is a different matter altogether," he said. "That calls for drastic measures."

"Anyway," Mosco said gruffly, "damned circus is coming apart at the seams. Too many clowns, by far. I think we may join up with another outfit next year."

Portia stood in the cool-edged evening air, reveling in the sheer absurdity, the unexpected thrill, of everything that had just happened. Gideon's hand had found hers, and he tapped her palm gently with one finger.

"Are you ready?" he asked.

"Yes," she replied. "Can we make one stop before we go?"

"Sure," said Mosco. "Where to?"

"The cemetery."

No one asked why. And when they arrived, no one followed her through the gate. They did not try to stop her tears when she knelt at Caroline's grave, or when she walked between the rows of empty graves behind Caroline, trailing her fingers across the tops of the headstones, saying goodbye. They did not hush her, or hold her, or tell her everything was as it should be. They knew better than that. They simply waited for her to return to them, wrapped her in a blanket, and drove into the ink-black night.

Her saviors.

Her family.

At last.

After All Is Said and Done

The August heat reminds everyone that the end of the season is not far away, the time of year when the circus makes the trip to winter quarters, and the carnival breaks apart like mercury.

Marie and Anna go home to their father, who is still throwing knives in the backyard, though he has to move his targets closer each year.

This year they are taking Mosco with them.

Polly and Pippa have tickets on the Atlantic Coast Line's Champion train to Miami with Mrs. Collington and Mrs. Murphy — they'll spend the winter working the indoor circuit, saving up their money for the house with the library. The Lucasies have a winter home in Gibsonton, but they'll be late going down this year, as Portia convinced them to employ the Kimble brothers to help find Violet.

"Everybody's lost someone," Short will tell them, as they reunite him with the business card he gave to Portia in the car. She has written a note on the back: *You never know who your next client might be.*

No one really knows where Jimmy goes, and Jim usually hibernates in a boarding house somewhere, but this year they got an offer for winter work at a movie studio in California that's making a series of short reels about human oddities. They both hate the idea of being filmed, but they couldn't pass up the money.

And Portia . . .

"You'll like New York," Gideon tells her. "I've never seen Jackal so excited to take someone back with him."

"I guess I still have a lot to learn about the bally," says Portia.

"Seems like the show doesn't change much, year to year, but there's always something new. New act, new route." He scuffs his shoe into the dust. "New friends."

She smiles. "I'll write to you in Boston."

"No," he says. Then he smiles, too. "Save your stories for when I see you."

"And when will that be?"

"I have some family business to take care of," he tells her. "It won't be long."

She has heard this before, from Max, from the others. Hollow promises echoing through the spaces between them, spoken by people who were already half-gone. But Gideon is different.

"I'll make sure you find me," he says.

Portia touches her shoe to Gideon's, to the place where he has been digging, and presses her toes to make an impression. Their tracks will not stay — they cannot hold against the elements and will be erased almost immediately by the unsettling August wind. But for now, their story is before them, printed in dust that only they can read.

And it is only the beginning.

PORTIA

Does the story start with how I got here? Does it start before that?

Lives begin only once. Stories are much more complicated. They can pick up, leave off, pick up again a thousand times. There is no beginning or end that way. And don't even get me talking about the middles.

But I have to start somewhere.

Begin at the beginning.

The first time I saw Gideon was on the lot, when I rode my stolen bicycle up to his truck and he was sitting in the bed and he looked like he hadn't slept in days. Which he hadn't.

Gideon says the first time was when the carnival passed us coming back from the graveyard. But he's wrong. That was the first time *he* saw *me*.

Gideon also says letting his route card fly out the window of his truck was an accident. I believe he's wrong about that, too. Because some things that look like accidents are really stories finding their own beginnings, and if I hadn't picked up that route card, how would I have known how to find the Wonder Show?

AUTHOR'S NOTE

Though most of the characters in this story, and all of the events that take place, are entirely fictional, several of the performers and human oddities whom Portia encounters are based on real people. After discovering such fascinating personalities and reading about their lives as performers, I found it impossible to resist casting them as part of Portia's story. I hope their fans and descendants forgive any liberties I have taken in adopting them to populate my novel.

The Lucasies—Rudolph, Antoinette, and Joseph—were a family of albinos "acquired" by P. T. Barnum in 1857 and exhibited for three years in Barnum's popular American Museum in New York City. They went on to tour with various circuses for another forty years, until Rudolph and Antoinette died unexpectedly in 1898. Joseph had learned to play the violin as a child and continued performing as "The Musical Albino" until his death in 1909. There is no record, however, of the Lucasies having a nonalbino daughter like Violet.

Jim is based on a variety of real-life giants, particularly Robert Wadlow and Jack Earle, both of whom were still alive when this story takes place. Both Wadlow and Earle were reluctant circus attractions, both appearing (though not together) as part of the Ringling Brothers show. Earle reportedly befriended several of the midgets who were part of the circus, and it was not uncommon for giants and midgets to become inseparable companions.

Polly and Pippa are based on Daisy and Violet Hilton, a very famous pair of conjoined twins who were born in England in 1908. They were managed throughout their childhood by unkind relatives motivated by financial gain; Daisy and Violet were eventually granted legal independence and went on to star in vaudeville shows and even played themselves in Tod Browning's movie *Freaks* in 1932. They made their final public appearance in Charlotte, North Carolina, in 1962 and were subsequently abandoned by the agent who had set up the show. Ever resourceful, Daisy and Violet found employment at a local grocery store, where they worked until their deaths from Hong Kong flu in 1969.

Arthur Plumhoff, who is mentioned in one of Jackal's stories, was a real performer known as The Human Pincushion and The Pain-Proof Man. There were also several real armless women like Marie, although none of them (as far as I know) had her talent for knife-throwing. Fat ladies, bearded ladies, dwarfs—all of these were standard fare in sideshows for decades. Other popular attractions were often people who suffered from birth defects or medical conditions. The Lobster Boy, for example, was a performer named Grady Stiles who was born in 1937 with a condition called ectrodactyly, which resulted in his fingers and toes being fused together to form clawlike extremities. Stiles and two of his four children toured together as The Lobster Family.

By 1939, when this story takes place, sideshows had largely fallen out of favor with the public. There was a new sense of discomfort, a feeling that paying money to look at human oddities was socially, and perhaps morally, inappropriate. However, one could argue that the sideshow provided a context for people who would otherwise have been marginalized or rejected by society to make a living, to survive and to form relationships with others who understood their point of view. Whether "freaks" were exploited or not is a question that has been and will continue to be debated for many years. Nonetheless, the era of the traveling circus and sideshow was a unique period in the history of American entertainment and provided countless stories that will be shared for generations to come.

The noblest art is that of making others happy.
  —P. T. Barnum

Acknowledgments

First and foremost, I must thank the Associates of the Boston Public Library for selecting me as their first Children's Writer-in-Residence and giving me the great gift of time, space, and financial support that allowed this novel to begin its existence.

Thanks also to Susan Bloom and Cathryn Mercier at the Center for the Study of Children's Literature at Simmons College, for opening the door to the field of children's literature, and to Anita Silvey, for showing me how many different paths awaited me.

To my advisors at Vermont College—for drawing stories out of me and teaching me to shape them.

To my editor, Kate O'Sullivan, for sharing her wisdom and guidance and for years of friendship that made working together more fun than a writer deserves.

To my family, especially my incomparable mother-in-law, Margaret Thomas Barnaby, for watching over my children with unparalleled love and patience while I hid at the library and worked on revisions.

And to Eddie, for making me get up early, for pouring the wine, for cheering me on, and for complicating my life in the most beautiful ways.